The Screenplay Series

CONTROL HOME

Control Home

AlbinoPigGorilla Press

For information:
www.meltoncartes.com
www.albinopiggorilla.com

ISBN: 979-8-9943732-2-4

Printed in the United States of America

This screenplay is part of
The Screenplay Series of published screenplays,
in paperback and e-book.

<u>CONTROL HOME</u>

an original screenplay

written by

Daniel Merritt

&

Melton Eduardo Cartes

FADE IN:

EXT. STREET - DAY

MALTEX FALOON, male, mid-thirties, wearing
a trench coat and mittens, is studying a
newspaper's classified section. He frowns
after scanning it and looks up. He starts
walking down the street.

A PUNK follows him. Maltex cuts through
a passageway partially obscured by steam
pluming from the street.

The punk hurries to catch up.

IN THE PASSAGEWAY

Hearing the punk's approach Maltex turns.

                    PUNK
          Give it up.

The punk holds his hand out impatiently.

                    MALTEX
          What?

                    PUNK
          Your wallet, asshole.

Maltex places his right hand reflexively on
his breast pocket.

                    MALTEX
          I haven't...got it...

The punk becomes furious and throws a
punch.

Maltex blocks it with his right FOREARM.
Then he drives his knee forward, into the
punk's gut. The punk sidesteps in time. He
throws a left hook.

Maltex blocks that with his right forearm
again and then elbows the punk in the face
with a left hook of his own.

The punk stumbles. Maltex advances and with his left elbow jabs him in the chest pushing him back.

Then he crosses with a right elbow and breaks the punk's nose producing a yelp from him.

The punk clips Maltex on the jaw with a flail and then clutches onto Maltex's right arm.

Maltex hits him again with his left elbow and tries to detach himself from the clinch.

With his nose bleeding profusely the punk desperately holds onto Maltex's right arm.

And then his right HAND.

Maltex lets out a howl. The fight goes out of him.

                    MALTEX (CONT'D)
          No. Stop. Stop.

The punk catches on. He grabs onto Maltex's right hand in earnest and Maltex drops to one knee.

The punk realizes that suddenly Maltex is no longer a threat. As he squeezes the hand Maltex collapses in excruciating pain. When he gets him on the ground he gives him a kick to the stomach.

There's nothing that Maltex can do.

The punk is enraged but also in pain, as he grimaces in anger his nose hurts him.

He reconsiders and then quickly reaches into Maltex's breast pocket.

He finds a money clip with a few bills, hardly enough for his trouble, and runs off after another kick.

Maltex rolls over and leans against a wall. He feels his breast pocket and then his coat pocket. From his coat pocket he partially pulls out his wallet. He relaxes.

INT. WAITING ROOM

Maltex, bruised and scuffed, is sitting quietly in the crowded waiting room of a doctor's office. He notices a well dressed woman nearby, with her arms in her lap. Her hands seem whithered prematurely for her age.

Maltex returns his attention to a magazine that he's doodling on. He grasps a stubby pencil in one mittened fist.

His doodling seems difficult and painful for him. He periodically stops and breathes. It's not clear what he's trying to draw. It looks like a clock...

A small window at the other end of the room slides open. A NURSE leans through the window. Behind her on a wall a digital clock reads 3:15 P.M.

>   NURSE
>   Faloon, Maltex. Two forty-
>   five.

>   MALTEX
>   That's me.

Maltex rises as he pushes himself out of the chair with hands that seem slightly curled in on themselves. He puts the stubby pencil in a pocket of his trench coat and walks toward a door to the right of the window.

INT. EXAMINATION-ROOM

The nurse stands to one side looking at
a file folder. The room has an extremely
antiseptic atmosphere about it.

Maltex has his coat off and is sitting on
the examination table. She gestures to his
hands with a scalpel.

                    NURSE
          I'm going to take the skin
          sample.

Maltex bites the leather mittens and winces
as he pulls them from his hands.

White, peeling, liver spotted, pasty skin
is revealed. Each hand is gnarled and
twisted in arthritic contortions. The nails
are yellowed and chipped. Small scars,
fresh scabs, and bruises cover the backs
of both hands. Purple and blue veins of
varying size crisscross the backs, yet
disappear in a very even line abruptly at
the wrists.

HIS HANDS LOOK LIKE THOSE OF AN EIGHTY
YEAR-OLD MAN. THE REST OF HIS FOREARMS
LOOK NORMAL.

The nurse scrapes the back of his right
hand with the scalpel. Maltex bites his
lip and then glares at her as she walks to
one of the workstations with the sample.
Odd grunts emanate from the nurse as she
conducts the tests.

                    MALTEX
          They've been hurting more.

The nurse grunts.

                    MALTEX (CONT'D)
          Doesn't seem to do anything
          anymore.

Maltex reaches into a pocket of his coat, pulls out a vial with a rubber stopper on the top.

                    MALTEX (CONT'D)
          Doesn't look right.

He holds the vial up, looking at it and showing it to the nurse's back.

                    MALTEX (CONT'D)
          Does that look right to
          you?

                    NURSE
               (over her shoulder)
          How often are you shooting
          up?

Maltex lowers the vial cradled in his palm to his lap.

                    MALTEX
          Depends on the pain.

The nurse turns toward Maltex and takes one of his hands. The vial drops into his lap.

His hands are more like fists, cupped in on themselves. She bends each finger back as far as they will go, until Maltex begins to grimace from the pain. None go very far. She rubs and massages each hand, testing and feeling each muscle and tendon.

She takes the vial from his lap, inspects the label.

                    NURSE
          This was out of date three
          days ago. You were supposed
          to come in then.

                    MALTEX
          I was on a job.

                    NURSE
          If you let it go bad, this
          stuff does more damage
          than good.
                    (pause)
          If you don't come in when
          you're scheduled to, the
          stuff's going to mutate.

The nurse moves away, opens a small
cabinet and drops the vial into a waste
receptacle. She turns and opens a cold
storage unit sitting on the counter and
takes out another vial.

She takes a wrapped syringe from a bin
that has a hand-scrawled sign taped above
it reading "FREE, TAKE SOME."

She tears open the wrapper and inserts the
needle into the rubber stopper on the new
vial and fills the syringe.

                    MALTEX
          I don't think that's it. It
          wasn't working very good
          before. Before it went
          bad I mean. The pain just
          never seems to go away
          entirely.

The nurse takes Maltex's left hand and
injects the needle between the knuckles of
his middle and ring fingers. Maltex winces.

                    NURSE
          Eighty-two percent of the
          nerve coatings in both
          hands have deteriorated
          permanently. You're in
          advanced neurological
          deterioration.

The nurse pulls the needle from the left
hand, refills it from the vial, and injects
the right hand.

                    NURSE (CONT'D)
          All the joints in your
          right hand and almost
          half of them in your
          left have swollen beyond
          the capability of the
          T-Butoxilina.

Finished, she throws the syringe into
the same trash receptacle she threw the
old vial into. She then picks up the file
folder and writes something.

                    MALTEX
          So what am I supposed to
          do? I can't work like this.

                    NURSE
               (over her shoulder)
          You've been told all along
          what you should do. Pick
          up a decent pair. These
          Welfares are garbage.

                    MALTEX
          I'm barely making the
          payments on the T-Bu. I
          can't afford anything else.

                    NURSE
          Do what you want. But the
          way you're pumping the
          stuff into them, they'll
          be gone in three months
          anyway, probably sooner.

Maltex pulls on his mittens and stands.

The nurse finishes writing in the file,
turns and hands him the itemized bill for
the shots. He looks at it with a grunt and
heads to the door to the waiting room.

He pauses a moment beside the door and
pulls an old, stained and crusted syringe
from one of his pockets. He hands it to

the nurse who drops it into the garbage
can.

He grabs a handful of packaged syringes
and stuffs them into his pocket and then
opens the door and steps out.

INT. WAITING ROOM

Maltex walks to the RECEPTIONIST and hands
him the bill. He takes it without looking
up and types a few commands into the
terminal, raises his hand and Maltex hands
him a credit card. He types in the card
number and waits.

Through an open door, behind the
receptionist, Maltex sees the woman with
the prematurely withered hands sitting at
an examination table.

A nurse has placed two BLACK BOXES on her
hands and flips a switch. She pulls the
boxes off, leaving black "cuffs" on the
remaining stumps. The withered hands are
gone.

The nurse returns with two other black
boxes that she fastens onto the cuffs. She
flips a switch and removes the boxes.

The woman now has beautiful, young hands,
appropriate to her age. She's thrilled and
flexes her new hands testing them.

Maltex is transfixed...

                    RECEPTIONIST
          This one's over limit.

He hands the card back. Maltex pulls out
three other cards.

He glances through the open door but the
woman is gone.

                    RECEPTIONIST (CONT'D)
          No good either.

Maltex hands him a third card.

                    MALTEX
          I haven't used it in a
          couple weeks. It might have
          something on it.

The receptionist checks this card.

                    RECEPTIONIST
          Nothing. Do you have a
          chip? I think we can still
          take those.

                    MALTEX
          No, I don't. Can't you just
          get around the limit?

                    RECEPTIONIST
          They're all way over. Amex,
          six hundred. Discover's
          revoked. I'm supposed to
          incinerate it.

The receptionist presses a button and a
flap slides up revealing a narrow slot in
the wall behind him. He starts to insert
the card into the slot.

                    MALTEX
          No!

Maltex tries to grab the card but merely
succeeds in hitting it to the floor and
causing himself pain.

                    RECEPTIONIST
          You can't use it anymore.

                    MALTEX
          Sorry. Just don't destroy it.

The receptionist looks at his trembling

hands and the pathetic look on his face,
then at the screen.

> MALTEX (CONT'D)
> What about the Amex? You
> said it was only over six
> hundred. You sure you can't
> push it a little farther?
> What's the worst that can
> happen? I'm the one who's
> going to get any flak if
> somebody pursues it.

The receptionist hands back the card and
takes the one Maltex holds out. He types
in a few commands and hands the card back.

> RECEPTIONIST
> There.

> MALTEX
> Thanks. I appreciate it.

Maltex turns to his right and leaves.

TITLES:

EXT. STREET - DAY

Fashions on the crowded street range from
business suits to the extremely casual, to
and past the point of decency.

Many of the people moving about have
peculiar physical characteristics. Some
lack a portion of their body, others have
mismatched limbs, etc.

Maltex steps out of the medical building
and turns left, loping carefully up the
street, his hands hidden in his pockets.

He passes small posters tacked up on walls
and light posts with an image of a happy
face with a Hitler mustache.

Maltex reaches a bus stop and stands next to a very dark-skinned African man dressed in a black leather Gestapo-like uniform. A bus pulls up to the corner. The door opens and they climb on.

A billboard on the side of the bus advertises a shop that handles "only the very finest" in male hands as well as male and female genitalia. The bus pulls away.

INT. POLICE STATION

The police station is like a horse track or the unemployment office. The air is thick with cigarette smoke. Throughout the room are uniformed police resembling Gestapo officers.

Almost everyone is watching an electronic ticker tape SIGN on one wall. Periodically people hurry over to wait in long lines for a bank of computer terminals.

Maltex enters and immediately gets in line for one of the terminals. He waits with his hands in his pockets watching the sign.

Maltex notices one item.

His turn arrives at the terminal. He types in commands and prints out a document, then takes the printout and makes his way across the room to another door.

INT. OFFICE

Maltex steps into a dark, musty room with a counter that runs from one end to the other. Along the counter are teller windows with signs that read; APPREHENSIONS - FETALS, APPREHENSIONS - SLAVING, etc.

Crowded noisy lines have formed at all the stations except for one, DONOR FRAUD.

Maltex goes to that station.

                    CLERK
          Can I help you?

Maltex hands her the printout.

                    MALTEX
          Faloon, Ident. 1184345. Just
          registered.

The clerk moves back into rows of shelves.
After a brief search she returns with a
thin legal-sized file to the counter.

                    CLERK
          Sign here and here.

Maltex glances at the file.

                    MALTEX
          Is this it?

                    CLERK
          That's all I have.

Maltex looks at the printout, points.

                    MALTEX
          It should be a lot thicker.

                    CLERK
          You'll have to access those
          yourself. This is all I
          have.

She shrugs and waits until Maltex painfully
signs.

                    CLERK (CONT'D)
          And I need your account
          number.

                    MALTEX
          640FIWT-DZ-282.

                    CLERK
          Down there for the retinal
          verification.

The clerk points to the end of the counter
where there are fragile-looking devices and
lines of people at them. Maltex moves to
the long but quickly moving lines for the
verification machines.

In front of him is RUTGER, another bounty
hunter. He's dressed much better than
Maltex but wears really thick glasses.

As the line moves forward, Maltex ignores
him, opens the file and begins perusing
it. The file is made up of photo facsimiles
and computer generated images of body
parts.

Rutger looks back after a few moments and
recognizes Maltex.

                    RUTGER
          Maltex! Whatcha got?

                    MALTEX
          D.F.

                    RUTGER
          Donor fraud? That money
          sucks. Skip tracing's
          better money.

Rutger tugs at his lapels showing off his
suit.

                    MALTEX
          I just gather evidence.

Maltex hesitates then looks at him
indicating his own hands. Rutger looks
at Maltex's mittens and then nods
uncomfortably.

                    RUTGER
          When you getting new ones?

                    MALTEX
                  (hesitates)
          I'm working on it.

                    RUTGER
          Yeah... So, what're the
          specs?

                    MALTEX
          This guy's posted
          practically every organ in
          his body at least a couple
          times and each time skipped
          out with the deposit money.
          You've got lips, tongue,
          arms, eyes, spleen, lungs...
          It goes on and on and on.

                    RUTGER
          He's got some balls.

                    MALTEX
          Seventeen, according to
          this...

Rutger chuckles and then opens his own
file. Maltex glances away.

A tall RED-HEADED, very curvaceous WOMAN
walks in carrying a courier package which
she takes to a clerk. She waits for the
clerk to return. She looks around the room
and notices Maltex. She looks at him.

                    MALTEX (CONT'D)
          Jesus...

                    RUTGER
          Huh? Oh. Yipes.

They both stare at the redhead as she
turns back to the clerk who returns with
another package for her. She nods at the

clerk and leaves.

Maltex and Rutger watch her go.

Rutger's turn comes up on one of the machines. He verifies and then moves towards the door.

                    RUTGER (CONT'D)
          See you later.

Maltex is next. He sticks his face up to one protuberance, hits a switch and a light moves across his eye.

He goes back to the clerk. She hands him a slip of paper with a number printed on it.

                    CLERK
          Here's your authorization
          code. Your log-in schedule
          is at 1400 hours every
          day. Failure to log-in
          deregisters you.

                    MALTEX
          Got it.

Maltex leaves.

INT. PHONE CUBICLE

BLASS GRIX, male, mid-forties, very well dressed, is speaking on a phone. The phone cubicle is on a sidewalk with a busy street as the backdrop.

                    PHIL
                (filtered)
          Is it a good stomach?

Blass pauses, shifts the phone to another hand. He has a tatoo on his right hand, between the thumb and index finger.

                    BLASS
          Yes. Very good. It's an
          iron stomach. Nothing
          upsets it.

                    PHIL
                 (filtered)
          Wonderful. Do you have
          scans you could show us?

Blass shakes his head and stifles a grunt.
The voice, Phil, sounds pathetically
excited.

                    BLASS
          Uh, yeah.

                    PHIL
                 (filtered)
          Lovely. When could you come
          by?

Blass checks his watch and smiles smugly.

                    BLASS
          Well...

INT. HALLWAY

Maltex stands outside one of many
apartment doors. He checks the number on
the door against one written in the file.
It matches. He presses a buzzer and waits.

A harsh VOICE blares out into the hallway
from a speaker beside the door.

                    VOICE
          What do you want?

                    MALTEX
          I'm here about the report
          you filed.

                         VOICE
              Have you found it?

                         MALTEX
              Couldn't tell you. I only
              heard about it yesterday.
              I'm following up.

A moment passes and then the door opens
revealing SWANSON SPINEMANN, a middle-aged
man supported by a crutch. He is wrapped
in some sort of blanket. His left leg is
missing.

                         SPINEMANN
              In, in. Have you found it?
              I've been waiting for days
              to hear back.

INT. SPINEMANN APARTMENT

Maltex enters, stepping past Spinemann,
into a light, airy octagonal room. The far
wall of the room has a window, each other
facet has a door. It is furnished in bright
colors.

Maltex looks at the doors, wondering where
they lead.

Spinemann closes the door behind him and
follows Maltex in. He motions for Maltex to
sit on a chair. He sits as well.

                         MALTEX
              Like I said, I don't really
              know. I need to ask you
              some questions.

                         SPINEMANN
              Why? I told them
              everything already. If
              you're just going to rehash
              what I've already said——

                    MALTEX
                 (interrupting)
          This won't take very long.
          I need you to identify
          some photos.

Maltex shuffles through the file folder and
pulls out a small stack of pictures. He
hands them to Spinemann.

Spinemann sits reluctantly looking through
the photos.

As he does, his eyes wander to Maltex's
leg. He absently flips the pages, no longer
paying attention to them.

Maltex notices but doesn't mention it.
Eventually Spinemann's gaze returns to the
pictures. He stops and pulls one out.

                    SPINEMANN
                 (cooing)
          This was his. God, it was
          beautiful.

Spinemann gets a wistful look on his
face and stares at the picture. One hand
caresses the picture. Maltex takes the
picture and looks at it.

                    MALTEX
          You're sure this was the
          one?

                    SPINEMANN
          No doubt. Look at the
          angles. The musculature on
          the inside of the thigh...
          I'll never forget it.

His eyes drift to Maltex's leg again.
Maltex writes a note in the file. Maltex
gestures to the other pictures in
Spinemann's hands.

                    MALTEX
          Any of the others look
          familiar?

Spinemann brings his gaze sharply up to
Maltex's face.

                    SPINEMANN
          Why? I said it was his.

                    MALTEX
          Whose though? Did you meet
          him? I mean, did you see
          the leg in person?

                    SPINEMANN
          No.

                    MALTEX
          I need to identify this
          guy. For all I know this
          folder could be twenty
          different guys. And I need
          to build a case against
          the specific person who
          defrauded you.

                    SPINEMANN
          But what happens to my
          leg?

                    MALTEX
          Well, it's not your leg. I
          suppose Hospital will break
          him down.

                    SPINEMANN
          I don't want Hospital
          getting its hooks into it.
          It's mine.

                    MALTEX
          I really don't know.

Maltex checks the file, paying little
attention to Spinemann. Spinemann eyes

Maltex's legs again.

                    SPINEMANN
                    (quietly)
          But it's mine.

Maltex looks up from the file.

                    MALTEX
          So you never saw his face?

                    SPINEMANN
          How much do you want for
          your leg?

Horrified, Maltex almost retracts his legs.

                    SPINEMANN (CONT'D)
          I'll give you fifteen for
          it.

                    MALTEX
          I'm not selling... How did
          this man get in touch with
          you?

He slumps in his chair a bit.

                    SPINEMANN
          Through a classified ad in
          the Gazette and the Post-
          Dispatch. I'd paid for a
          week, but he responded to
          it the first day.

                    MALTEX
          Did you list your phone
          number or address?

                    SPINEMANN
          The newspaper voicemail. He
          called and left his number.

                    MALTEX
          Do you still have it?

Spinemann looks at Maltex calmly, as if he knows some secret. He reaches under his blanket and takes out a piece of paper.

He hands it to Maltex.

                    SPINEMANN
          I want that back.

Maltex nods. He copies down the number and hands the paper back to Spinemann, who pockets it carefully.

                    MALTEX
          What did the ad say?

                    SPINEMANN
          That I was looking for a
          leg in good condition. How
          much I wanted to pay. And
          the voicemail number.

                    MALTEX
          Did he ever say why he'd
          picked your ad?

                    SPINEMANN
          No. Just that he ran across
          it.

                    MALTEX
          Why was he selling his leg?
          Wasn't he still using it?

Spinemann pulls back the blanket. His left leg has been surgically removed at his hip.

                    SPINEMANN
          I didn't care. I want to
          walk. I don't give a shit
          about anything else.

Maltex pulls pictures out from different sub-sections of the file, indicating various victims.

Photos of the same leg. He shows them to
Spinemann.

                    MALTEX
          They're all the same. He
          wasn't going to sell you
          anything. He's got your
          same piece optioned five
          times right here.

Spinemann takes them and looks through
them. He frowns as he recognizes the leg.

Spinemann stares mutely at the pictures,
then at Maltex.

                    SPINEMANN
          Well, I was planning on
          stiffing him on the rest of
          the payment anyway. He did
          seem like a slime.

Maltex nods at him, replaces the pictures,
closes the folder and rises.

                    MALTEX
          If he's found and he still
          has the limb, you might be
          notified, but don't count
          on it.

As Maltex stands there, Spinemann's
expression changes. He eyes Maltex's legs,
nearly licking his lips.

                    SPINEMANN
          Eighteen hundred.

Maltex watches the old man warily, almost
with disgust. Maltex starts to leave the
room. He barks his shin on a coffee table.
Spinemann flinches.

                    SPINEMANN
          Two thousand. I'll give you
          two thousand.

Spinemann scrambles to his foot, reaching out for Maltex. Maltex is scowling from the pain to his shin.

                    SPINEMANN
          Right now. Two grand.
          Whattaya say?

                    MALTEX
          I've got to go now.

Spinemann stumbles and lunges for support on Maltex. He falls clutching one of Maltex's hands. Maltex shrieks from the pain and yanks away.

                    SPINEMANN
          You're not careful. You
          don't care like I do.

Spinemann hits the floor. He hugs one of Maltex's legs.

                    SPINEMANN
          No, don't go! I'll take
          care of it.

Maltex drags the dead weight out the door.

                    MALTEX
          Get OFF!

                    SPINEMANN
          Twenty ONE hundred!

Maltex gets outside, in the hallway. He tries to yank free. The file falls on the floor as he tends to his left hand.

                    SPINEMANN
          Don't go!

                    MALTEX
          Get OFF ME!

Maltex kicks Spinemann in the face.

Spinemann whimpers and lets go.

Maltex steps away from Spinemann, disgusted. He struggles to collect the file and all the scattered documents.

He finally leaves, clumsily.

EXT. STREET - NIGHT

FLEXIBEE BOLD, the redhead Maltex saw at the assignment office, is walking downstairs from an elevated train station, wearing a raincoat and a hat that are wet from the drizzle.

She proceeds down the sidewalk to a posh hotel. As she enters, men around her stare. Her figure is impossible to hide even in a masculine looking raincoat.

She walks on ignoring her surroundings.

INT. HOTEL LOBBY

Flex walks to the bank of elevators and presses the call button. She stands impassively.

INT. HALLWAY

Flex walks down the hall looking for a hotel room. She glances at each door she passes.

She finds the room and pauses outside the door, staring at it. She squints at the door as if it holds some danger.

She knocks on the door. It opens. Blass Grix is standing there. He smiles at her.

                    BLASS
          Hey, Flex.

Without saying anything Flex makes a
questioning expression, as if asking "So?
Where is it?". Blass puts his hands up
placatingly.

                    BLASS
          I've encountered some minor
          obstacles. But <u>don't</u> worry.

Flex listens and then sighs dramatically,
looks away. She seems skeptical, but not
particularly surprised.

                    BLASS
          However. There is something
          <u>you could do</u> that might
          help <u>both of us</u>.

Flex stares at him, contemplating. Finally
she whips her hat off in one motion and
steps into the hotel room in another.

Once inside she tosses the hat aside and
whips the raincoat off. She's wearing a red
wraparound dress tied around the waist.
The sight is magnificent. The neckline
plunges precipitously while the skirt
tantalizingly opens revealing a thigh.

Blass smiles salaciously and closes the
door.

INT. BLIND MAN'S HOME

Maltex is standing at the open front door
while TUCHO, a blind man welcomes him.
Maltex looks inside the man's apartment.
It's completely dark, except for streetlight
shining in.

                    TUCHO
          Come in.

                    MALTEX
          Uh, sure.

As Maltex steps inside Tucho moves him aside to close the door. With the door closed Maltex can't see.

The blind man moves away from him. He seems to go to another room.

                    TUCHO (O.S.)
          So what is it you want
          from me...?

Maltex is stranded.

                    MALTEX
          Uh, actually. Um do you
          have a light? In here? I
          can't see anything.

Maltex tries to get around but promptly bangs into something.

                    TUCHO
          Oh sorry. Hang on!

The blind man comes back.

                    TUCHO
          I forget that some people
          can see. There's a switch
          over here somewhere.

                    MALTEX
          I think I tried that one.

                    TUCHO
          Oh, it doesn't work?

Tucho tries the switch a couple of times.

                    MALTEX
          No, it's dead.

                    TUCHO
          Well, there's a lamp over
          here.

Tucho finds a lamp that works. Maltex

sighs, relieved.

                    TUCHO
          Alright, follow me.

Maltex follows Tucho into the dark kitchen.

                    TUCHO
          Can you see the table?

                    MALTEX
          Yeah.

                    TUCHO
          Have a seat.

Maltex sits down while Tucho fumbles with
a lamp over the kitchen table. He places
his hand on the bulb and pulls the chain.
The light comes on. Tucho can feel the
heat from the bulb. He smiles victoriously.

TUCHO moves about the kitchen making
coffee. He's very sure of his movements.

Maltex opens the case file.

                    MALTEX
          Can you tell me what his
          voice sounded like?

Tucho listens.

                    TUCHO
          Soft. Singsongy. Very
          assured.

Tucho hums a bit to try to demonstrate.

                    TUCHO
          Actually I have a recording.
                    (pause)
          Coffee?

                    MALTEX
          Fine, thank you. A recording?

He pours a cup of coffee and places
it before Maltex. Maltex takes a sip,
grimaces, puts it down, and opens the case
file.

                    TUCHO
          I make shitty coffee, don't I?

Maltex is caught off guard.

                    MALTEX
          No, it's fine.

                    TUCHO
          That's okay. You don't have
          to drink it. Anyway...

Tucho reaches into his pocket and pulls
out a small disk.

                    TUCHO
          It's a recording from my
          telephone security system.
          A copy. I make one of
          everyone that calls me. It
          helps me remember people.

Maltex takes the recording.

                    MALTEX
          Can I have it?

                    TUCHO
          Yeah, that's why I copied it.

                    MALTEX
          This could help quite a bit.
          Thanks.
                    (pauses)
          Incidentally, did this guy
          give a reason why he was
          giving up his eyes?

Tucho shrugs.

                    TUCHO
          No. He was just giving
          up one eye. Better than
          nothing.

                    MALTEX
          How was the transfer going
          to take place?

                    TUCHO
          I gave him an access
          code to a subset of my
          credit account. Two-thirds
          payment up front with the
          remainder to be paid after
          implantation.

Maltex snorts and shakes his head.

                    TUCHO
          Don't give me that attitude.

Again, Maltex is surprised by the blind
man.

                    MALTEX
                (contrite)
          It just seems to me, like a
          long shot...working through
          a guy like this.

                    TUCHO
          Of course it was.
                (pause)
          But I can afford long
          shots. What if it worked
          out? I'd be looking you in
          the eyes right now, instead
          of picturing you with a
          blue and yellow houndstooth
          sportscoat and a shiny,
          bald head.

Maltex visualizes that tableau.

                    MALTEX
          I suppose. So, is there
          anything else you can tell me?

                    TUCHO
          Nope.

The blind man mopes and shakes his head.
Maltex stares at him uncomfortably.

INT. MALTEX'S LIVINGROOM

Maltex's apartment is simple and drab,
furnished in dark tones. It's very
cluttered by clothes, dishes and videotape
cassettes. Maltex has good taste and used
to have the money for it.

He has a VCR and television, both of which
are on. The sound coming from them is of
billiard balls being hit.

Maltex is sitting on his couch carefully
taping the last part to a patchwork made
of scans of ears, eyes, nose, lips, etc.
He flips a piece of tracing paper over the
top and lightly draws a vague outline to
the resulting face.

There is a drink perched on the table
before him.

He shakily injects his hands with the
T-Butoxilina. He withdraws the needle and
pauses a moment, his whole body shaking
with the pain, waiting for it to take
effect.

The pain subsides somewhat. He flexes his
hands and grimaces, the pain has not gone
away entirely.

He picks up a pad and pen resting beside
him and writes, slowly forming each word.

INSERT:
5. REPORT ON SPINEMANN
6. SPINEMANN PHONE RECORDS.
7. FOLLOW UP CONNECTIONS BETWEEN VICTIMS

                                        CUT TO:

Each stroke of the pencil is agony. He periodically takes a break and looks up at the television.

On screen is a professional pool tournament. The player, obviously winning by a huge margin and showing off a bit, is a younger and successful looking Maltex. A videotape.

The cassette case sits on top of the television. The label gives the title of the tournament, the date, and the location. Other cassettes lying about have similar names and dates on them.

Maltex is lost in thought. He eventually falls asleep, the write-up incomplete on his lap, and the tape still running.

INT. PHONE CUBICLE - DAY

Maltex inserts his credit chip. He's tired.

He types his ID number and the screen flashes...

INSERT:
You have thirty seconds to log-in: Counting! PASSWORD VERIFICATION

                                        CUT TO:

He types in the case authorization code. The countdown blinks off.

Maltex types in his report about the case so far, the time spent, and his progress. His account balance adjusts.

He now uses the terminal in a more
leisurely manner.

INSERT:
Request phone records: Spinemann, Swanson

Lists scroll across the screen.

                              CUT TO:

Maltex scans it. He slows the scroll and
inspects the list more closely.

Maltex sorts the list into incoming and
outgoing calls and cross-references them to
eliminate dead-ends.

He is left with just a few, all from the
same number.

An update on the case appears. Two new
victims have turned up.

He notes the phone number of one of the
two newest victims, a woman named FLEXIBEE
BOLD, when it flashes on the screen.

He dials.

                    OPERATOR
                   (filtered)
          Frye and Cooke Insurance,
          may I help you?

                    MALTEX
          I'm trying to locate an
          employee named Flexibee Bold.

                    OPERATOR
                   (filtered)
          She's not in today.

                    MALTEX
          Do you have her home phone
          number or address? It's
          important that I get in
          touch with her.

                    OPERATOR
                   (filtered)
          I can't give out her——

                    MALTEX
                 (interrupting)
          Faloon, Ident. 640tdz282.
          Column authority, class-B.

                    OPERATOR
                   (filtered)
          Very well... Here's the
          number.

He prints out that information. Then he
types in commands to print out the missing
reports and body part scans in the case
file.

The phone cubicle starts spitting out
printouts in an adjacent tray. The screen
indicates that the printing cost is being
deducted from his pay on the case.

Maltex watches each page come out until
the printer jams.

Maltex jabs at buttons. He hits the cubicle
with his elbow a few times. Nothing.

Finally, he collects the successful
printouts and leaves.

EXT. FLEXIBEE'S HOUSE - DAY

Maltex is standing on the front stoop of
a plain brownstone. He presses the buzzer
beside the door.

After a moment the door swings open.

FLEXIBEE BOLD stands in the doorway,
wearing another outfit that really
accentuates her stunning figure. Maltex
stands, dumbstruck for a few moments as he

recognizes her.

                    MALTEX
          Uh...uh. I'm, uh Maltex...
          Maltex Faloon...

Flex stares at him quietly. She seems
impatient, annoyed.

                    MALTEX
          I'm looking for...

Maltex clumsily checks his notes. His eyes
keep drifting to take in her figure.

                    MALTEX
          ...um, Flexibee Bold?

                    FLEX
          FLEX!

She nods at him. Maltex steps back. Her
voice is a shock. It is a metallic grating
sound.

Flex seems reluctant to speak.

                    MALTEX
          Is that you?

Flex nods.

                    MALTEX
          Oh,...I'm here about the
          report you filed. Follow
          up. Get an ID. That kind of
          thing.

                    FLEX
          Didn't my report cover
          everything?

                    MALTEX
          ...Basic stuff, yeah. I
          just want to get as much
          background as I can. Make

          my job easier.

                    FLEX
          How long?

                    MALTEX
          ...Just a few clarifications.
          Half an hour maybe.

After a moment Flex steps back to allow
Maltex in.

                    MALTEX
          Thank you.

INT. FLEXIBEE'S HOUSE

The colors are warm and muted and the
furniture appears extremely comfortable.

Flex sits on a couch and motions for
Maltex to sit opposite her on a chair.

Maltex tears his eyes from Flex to look
through the file. He flips through the
pages with difficulty.

                    MALTEX
          Just a minute. Um, I have
          it here somewhere.

He fumbles about. Smiles at her. Stares.

                    MALTEX
          You were dealing with him
          for...uh.

Still searches. Flex watches him,
impatiently. She notices his mittens.

                    FLEX
                 (irritated)
          For my voice.

That startles Maltex.

                    MALTEX
          What?!?

                    FLEX
          I <u>want</u> a new <u>larynx</u>.

He regains his composure.

                    MALTEX
          Right...

Maltex looks around the room and notices
framed photographs of a younger Flex
singing on stage at a school function,
a pageant, in a radio station, etc.
He glances back at her with more
understanding...

                    MALTEX
          ...He skipped after you
          paid him twelve-seventy in
          front money.

                    FLEX
          That's <u>in</u> the report.

                    MALTEX
          Did he have current
          medicals?

She nods at him.

                    MALTEX
          Why was he selling?

                    FLEX
          I wasn't buying his voice.

                    MALTEX
          Oh. He was brokering?

Flex nods at him again.

Maltex makes some notes painfully in his
file. Flex watches him struggle. He pulls
several photos from the file and hands

them to Flex.

                    MALTEX
          Any of these look familiar?

Flex looks them over. She takes her time
and picks two or three. But then she hands
them back and shrugs.

                    FLEX
          Lips...ear. Maybe.

Maltex waits for possibly more. Flex
remains silent.

                    MALTEX
          You, uh...don't like to
          talk.

Flex looks at him and frowns. Maltex looks
down, then back at her.

                    FLEX
          Latent Degeneracy.

                    MALTEX
          Excuse me?

Flex points at her throat.

                    FLEX
          Pretty common.

                    MALTEX
          Yeah.

Maltex smiles, makes notes in the file.

                    FLEX
          I don't like it.

Flex looks at him for a few moments and
then points at her throat again. Then her
face changes.

                    FLEX
          I'm sorry. All this makes

                    me feel stupid. I can't
                    believe...

Maltex looks up and leans forward. Flex
sits thinking for a few moments. She
finally shakes her head.

                    FLEX
               Do you really think any of
               this is going to be of any
               use?

Flex stares at him with tears forming in
her eyes. Maltex gulps quietly. Although
this makes him nervous, he smiles, trying
to console her.

                    MALTEX
               It might.

She leans back, takes out a cigarette and
lights it. She puffs and smiles at him.

                    MALTEX
               How did you contact him?

Flex leans forward, grabs a newspaper,
flips it open to the classifieds and points
at an ad. Maltex reads it.

                    MALTEX
               How long did you run this
               ad?

She puffs, thinking.

                    FLEX
               I run it continuously.

Maltex is surprised by that answer but
then he sees the photographs again.

                    FLEX
               It's not everyday you find
               a good larynx.

                    MALTEX
          I suppose so. Can you
          describe him?

                    FLEX
          Dark hair. Regular looking.
          I don't know... Well
          dressed.

Maltex nods slowly and resigns himself.

                    FLEX
          Is there going to be
          anything else?

Maltex smiles at her and shakes his
head. He collects his papers slowly, with
difficulty, and rises.

                    MALTEX
          No, that's it for now. I'll
          get in touch if I need
          anything more.

She stands to let him out. He glances at
her figure again. She notices but doesn't
seem to mind.

                    MALTEX
          If you hear from him or
          remember anything, please
          call me.

Maltex winces as he slowly fishes out a
business card and hands it to her.

She accepts it pleasantly and then shakes
hands with him. Maltex jumps from the pain
of the handshake.

                    FLEX
          Sorry.

                    MALTEX
          That's alright.

Flex shakes his hand more gently.

                    FLEX
          Thank you.

That surprises Maltex a little. He smiles,
nods and leaves.

EXT. STREET - MAGIC

Maltex is walking down a busy street. He's
lost in thought, presumably about Flex.

He stops at a kiosk and buys a newspaper.
He opens it to the classifieds and looks
for her ad.

INSERT:
WANTED: New Larynx, F, good cond. any age.
Current meds. Mailbox 424-b73.

There are a lot of "Wanted" ads for body
parts on the pages Maltex is looking at.
He drops his head depressed by that.

He continues walking and passes a store
with a turquoise facade and blue neon sign:
BELOTZ ORGANICS.

He stops to look in the windows. The glass
is wire reinforced. Inside, on display, are
large glass cylinders holding various body
parts; a leg, an arm, eyes, ears, genitals
and hands.

Maltex steps closer to look at the case
holding the pair of male hands. The
fluid the body parts are in is highly
oxygenated. Tiny bubbles cling to the hair
and skin.

Maltex stares at the hands. A hand-painted
sign nearby says, "FINANCING AVAILABLE".

                    VOICE
          Nice pair! Huh?

Maltex starts. He looks up. A man is standing in the door, looking at him.

>   MALTEX
>   Uh, yes...

The man grabs Maltex gently by the arm and leads him inside.

>   BELOTZ
>   I'm Mr. Belotz. Here. Take
>   a closer look.

>   MALTEX
>   I can't...

BELOTZ takes the case from the display and places it on a counter top covered with felt.

>   BELOTZ
>   These are Bio-Generated and
>   Sync-Exercised hands. Not
>   remnants.

>   MALTEX
>   Sync Exercised?

>   BELOTZ
>   They're pristine. Never
>   belonged to anyone. They
>   were generated at the
>   Hewson/Badillo plant
>   and exercised by robot
>   control to develop that
>   handsome musculature you
>   see there. Sync-Exercising
>   is a unique Hewson/Badillo
>   feature. They take the
>   proto-appendage and use
>   a carefully, computer-
>   monitored regime to
>   "develop" the appendage to
>   optimum performance and
>   health.

Maltex squints slightly.

                    BELOTZ
          Normal native hands aren't
          as healthy as these. You
          should see the plant. All
          these tanks with these
          hands wiggling away.
          Exercising.

Belotz acts out the hands "exercising".

                    BELOTZ
          May I?

Belotz takes Maltex's free hand and pulls
the mitten off...

                    MALTEX
          No, please——

...before Maltex can stop him.

                    BELOTZ
          Oh. What do we have here?
          I see.

Maltex is stymied. Embarrassed.

                    MALTEX
          They're uh...Welfares...
          They're old.

                    BELOTZ
          You know, if you don't
          replace these soon, the
          decrepitude can spread to
          healthy tissue.

Maltex yanks his arm away from Belotz. He
glares at him.

Belotz meets his glare with a maddeningly
calm and superior gaze. He even smiles
slightly.

                    BELOTZ
          What would you say if
          I told you I could put
          you and these new hands
          together today for just
          three hundred and fifty
          DMs?

Maltex seems to almost lunge at the idea
of having those healthy hands instead. His
eyes water a little.

                    MALTEX
          How, how could you do that?

                    BELOTZ
          Easily. With our financing
          program.

                    MALTEX
          Three fifty?

                    BELOTZ
          Sure. Come have a seat
          over here.

Belotz motions Maltex to sit at a desk with
him. He takes out a credit application and
a pen.

                    BELOTZ
          Fill this form out and we
          can get you started.

Maltex stares at the form. Just looking at
the form causes him pain. Belotz notices.

                    BELOTZ
          Tell you what. As long as
          you sign it I can fill it
          out for you.

Belotz places the pen in Maltex's right
hand. Maltex reads the form.

                    MALTEX
          Where is the price? The
          three fifty?

                    BELOTZ
          Right here is the
          itemization.

Belotz points at a paragraph.

                    BELOTZ
          With a credit deposit of
          twenty five hundred you
          qualify for a monthly
          payment of three fifty.

Maltex looks up at Belotz shaken by the
numbers.

                    MALTEX
          Monthly payments? What's
          the total?

                    BELOTZ
          The total is right here.
          Nine years equals thirty
          five thousand, plus the
          twenty eight percent
          interest on the credit
          line. It works out to
          something like forty two
          thousand five.

Maltex gasps audibly. Belotz just looks at
him.

                    MALTEX
          Forty two thousand
          deutschemarks?

                    BELOTZ
          Yes.
                    (pause)
          Which credit card would
          you like to use for your
          deposit?

                    MALTEX
          I can't. I don't have
          enough credit. I'm maxed
          out.

                    BELOTZ
          You don't have twenty five
          hundred in credit?

                    MALTEX
     No.

Maltex gets up abruptly. He stumbles away
from the desk.

                    BELOTZ
          Hey? Where ya' going?

                    MALTEX
          I've got to go.

Belotz follows Maltex to the door. He steps
in his way smiling.

                    BELOTZ
          Don't you want those hands?

                    MALTEX
          ...Of course...

                    BELOTZ
                 (cloyingly)
          What are you waiting for?

For Maltex the emotional strain is too
much to bear. He leaves.

INT. PHONE CUBICLE - NIGHT

Maltex is sitting in a phone cubicle. He
dials up the police department records. A
log-in routine appears on the screen.

Maltex types in his identification and case
authorization code.

INSERT:
You have thirty seconds to log-in:
Counting! PASSWORD VERIFICATION

He types in the case authorization code.
The countdown blinks off.

The screen comes to life, listing all
his actions so far on the case and his
compensation.

INSERT:
COMPENSATION: $132.57.

He begins typing in information.

INSERT:
7:30 QUESTIONED VICTIM FLEXIBEE BOLD RE:
DEAL WITH SUSPECT. POSITIVE I.D. ON SEVERAL
BODY PARTS.

MEMO: PLACE ADS IN SECTOR NEWSPAPERS.

EXT. STREET

Maltex is in the back of a cab with the
door open and his feet on the sidewalk.
He looks exhausted. He has one mitten
off. He is giving himself an injection of
T-Butoxilina.

The cab driver crosses the street to the
cab as Maltex pulls the needle from his
hand and slips it back into his pocket.

                    CABBIE
          How's the case?

                    MALTEX
          Fun as ever.

CABBIE stands there lighting a corncob
pipe. From the way his pants sag
dramatically on one side, it appears half
of his butt is missing.

                    MALTEX
          Just taking a break right
          now.

Cabbie watches Maltex carefully flex his
hand and slip his mitten back on.

                    CABBIE
          When are you getting new
          ones?

Maltex shakes his head and chuckles.

                    MALTEX
          I'm working on it.

Maltex looks at him, then at his hands.

                    CABBIE
          Yeah, well. The guys
          haven't seen you in a
          while. You want to come
          hang out?

                    MALTEX
               (tired)
          Don't think so. I've got to
          work.

Maltex rises.

                    CABBIE
          Have you thought
          anymore about that deal
          of my cousin's? The
          telemarketing?

                    MALTEX
          The skin products?

                    CABBIE
          Yeah.

                    MALTEX
          Nah, Cabbie. I can't do
          that.

                    CABBIE
          Why not? He says you can
          make from fifteen to four
          grand starting out. Easy.

Maltex looks at him dubiously.

                    MALTEX
          Why don't you do it?

Cabbie points at his head.

                    CABBIE
          Tinnitus. Bad ears. Can't
          be on the phone for very
          long...
                    (pause)
          But you could. They got
          headsets so you wouldn't
          have to hold the phone...

Maltex shakes his head slightly.

                    MALTEX
          It's just not me, Cabbie. I
          wouldn't be good at that.
          I've got to believe in what
          I'm doing...

Cabbie looks at Maltex, as if to respond,
but stops himself, disappointed.

                    CABBIE
          Well. If you're ever
          interested...

Maltex smiles at him.

                    CABBIE
          Where you off to now?

                    MALTEX
          The Post-Dispatch.

Cabbie gets in behind the wheel of the
cab, looking back.

                    CABBIE
          Get in. Freebie.

                    MALTEX
          Sure? Gee, thanks.

                    CABBIE
          Don't mention it.

Maltex climbs into the cab and manages to
close his door. Cabbie turns to look at
Maltex.

                    CABBIE
          I mean it. Don't mention
          it...to anybody.

He winks at him.

INT. CLASSIFIED ADS OFFICE

Maltex stands at a counter that divides
the room into a waiting area and an office
area.

He's filled out a card with a grid of boxes
on one side.

INSERT:
WHITE MALE SEEKS TONGUE IN GOOD CONDITION.
WILLING TO PAY EXTRA FOR ADDED DEXTERITY,
SENSITIVITY, AND LENGTH. MEDICALS MUST BE
CURRENT. BOX 2234. LEAVE MESSAGE.

                                   CUT TO:

Maltex reads it to himself.

A clerk approaches him and takes the card.
She checks it over before she types the
information into a terminal behind the
counter.

                    CLERK
          Once is fifteen dollars.
          Twice, twenty-five. After

                    that it's ten dollars a
                    day.

                              MALTEX
                    Do two days.

Maltex pulls out two pinkish, twelve-fifty
bills from his pocket and hands them to
the clerk.

                              CLERK
                    It'll start running
                    at midnight, and end
                    at midnight day after
                    tomorrow.

INT. FLEX'S OFFICE/PHONE CUBICLE INTERCUT -
MORNING

Flexibee sits at a terminal, wearing a
headset. She is busy typing information
into a computer. Although the overhead
lighting makes her skin look pasty she's
still a knockout.

                              BLASS
                         (filtered)
                    You find anything more on
                    that hunter?

                              FLEX
                    No "Hello"?
                         (pause)
                    He stopped by my house
                    yesterday.

                              BLASS
                         (filtered)
                    What'd you tell him?

                              FLEX
                    Just your name, what you
                    look like, and where you're
                    staying.

                    BLASS
                  (filtered)
          What!?

                    FLEX
          That's the first time I've
          heard any emotion from you
          since I met you.

                    BLASS
                  (filtered)
          Damn you. I practically
          shit my pants.
                  (pause)
          Does he have any real
          leads?

                    FLEX
          Nah. Nuthin'. I got the
          impression the way I look
          was really throwing him
          off.

                    BLASS
                  (filtered)
          That's easy to understand.
          You're pretty distracting.
          But what does he have for
          real?

                    FLEX
          Thank you very much. Why
          don't <u>you</u> tell <u>me</u> what
          progress <u>you've</u> made <u>first</u>?

PHONE CUBICLE

Blass looks irritated, but his voice
betrays nothing.

                    BLASS
          I don't have anything yet.
          It won't be too much longer
          though. I really need
          you to keep tabs on this

                    hunter. If you keep him
                    off my tail, it'll make it
                    a lot easier for me to get
                    you what you want.

                         FLEX
                    (filtered)
          Why?

                         BLASS
          Why what?

                         FLEX
                    (filtered)
          Why would it make it
          easier?

                         BLASS
          Well shit, Flex. How am I
          supposed to get you a new
          voice from the joint?

                         FLEX
                    (filtered)
          You said he couldn't touch
          you. What are you worried
          about?

                         BLASS
          He can't touch me because
          I'm careful.

FLEX'S OFFICE

                         BLASS
                    (filtered)
          This way I can keep a step
          ahead of him.

Flex doesn't seem to like the conclusion
that leads her to.

                         BLASS
                    (filtered)
          See, if I know he's going

to zig, I know I should
zag.

                    FLEX
Right.

                    BLASS
               (filtered)
So what does he have?

                    FLEX
He's got all the medical
scans you gave to those
people.

                    BLASS
               (filtered)
That's fine.

                    FLEX
What about the DNA files?

PHONE CUBICLE

                    BLASS
I substituted different
information before I gave
out those scans. Does
he have a description or
police drawing?

                    FLEX
               (filtered)
No. He did ask me what you
looked like.

                    BLASS
And?

                    FLEX
               (filtered)
I told him you're blond and
a slob.

Blass smiles.

                    BLASS
          Good girl. That'll throw
          him for a while. Alright, I
          need you to keep in close
          contact with him.

                    FLEX
                    (filtered)
          How close?

                    BLASS
          Well, don't go breakin' my
          heart now, Babe. You're my
          number one. You know, make
          friends with him.

                    FLEX
                    (filtered)
          Friends.

                    BLASS
          Yeah... And one more thing.

FLEX' OFFICE

Flex sighs and looks very doubtful.

INT. NOODLE BAR - DAY

Maltex steps into a crowded noodle bar.
People are standing, eating their lunches
at small shelves opposite the counter where
people are seated and eating.

The restaurant owner, Maury, an older man,
notices Maltex and brightens up happily.

                    MAURY
          Maltex! Welcome.

Maury comes out from behind the counter to
greet Maltex.

                    MAURY
          Hungry?

                    MALTEX
          Hi, Maury. Yes, I'm starved.

                    MAURY
          Hold on a moment.

Maury looks around and sees someone at the
counter leaving a seat next to the wall.

                    MAURY
          Right here, Maltex.

A man waiting to be seated steps forward.

                    MAN
          Hey, I've been waiting--

                    MAURY
             (interrupting)
          I'm sorry, he phoned ahead.
          He made a reservation.

                    MAN
          Reservation?

Maury steers Maltex to the vacated seat. He
clears the plates, puts a new place setting
in front of him.

The man gives up.

                    MAURY
          We got a good special
          today.

                    MALTEX
          Thanks, Maury.

Maltex looks at the menu as Maury walks
away.

Maltex slowly takes his mittens off. A
woman eating next to him notices and
averts her eyes. Maltex frowns.

Maltex picks up chopsticks from the
counter, unwraps them and then tries to

break them apart. He can't get a good grip
on them to get leverage enough to split
them.

Maury returns, behind the counter again.

                    MAURY
          Know what you want, Maltex?

                    MALTEX
          Uh...

Maury takes the chopsticks from Maltex and
splits them apart effortlessly. He hands
them back.

Maltex smiles at him.

                    MALTEX
          Thanks, Maur'. I'll have
          the special.

                    MAURY
          Good choice.

Maury turns to the kitchen.

                    MAURY
          Special on twelve.

He turns back to Maltex.

                    MAURY
          I saw Tony Ha Ha a couple
          weeks ago.

                    MALTEX
          Ha Ha? What's he up to?

                    MAURY
          He's still hustling. He
          says he's in a tournament
          coming up.

                    MALTEX
          The Agfa?

                    MAURY
          I don't remember.

                    MALTEX
          Well that's the next one.

Maury looks at Maltex, surprised that he
would know that.

                    MAURY
          You still following it?

Maltex shrugs.

                    MAURY
          Yeah, well he was talking
          big, as usual.

                    MALTEX
          Yep', funny guy.

                    MAURY
          Always making laughable
          bets.

                    MALTEX
          Right.

Maltex chuckles at that last comment.
Maury glances at Maltex's hands.

                    MAURY
          I remember that time you
          and him squared off in the
          Buckeye Tournament. God,
          that was great. You were
          slick. I won twenty-five
          hunnerd off you that time.

Maltex nods, remembering.

                    MALTEX
          That was a while ago.

                    MAURY
          How are your hands, Maltex?

Maltex becomes guarded, wary. He shrugs.

                    MALTEX
          There's not much to say
          about them.

                    MAURY
          Any luck getting new ones?

Maltex looks away. Then he looks up at
Maury. Maury is a kind friend and only
means well.

Maltex smiles at him forlornly.

                    MALTEX
          'Fraid not. I can't afford
          them.

Maury is saddened by that. He's at a loss
for words.

                    MAURY
          I wish I could help you,
          Maltex——

                    MALTEX
                  (interrupting)
          Don't worry about me,
          Maury. I'll figure it out.

He smiles at the avuncular man.

                    MALTEX
          Thanks, tho'.

A waitress brings Maltex's order and hands
it over the counter. Maury helps place it
in front of Maltex.

                    MAURY
          Ah, here you go.
                  (pause)
          Well, let me know if you
          need anything. Enjoy.

Maury steps away to leave Maltex in peace.

Maltex gingerly tests the chopsticks and then the big soup spoon in the bowl.

It doesn't look like it'll be easy.

EXT. HOUSE - DAY

Maltex is checking an address written in his folder against the address on the house.

Satisfied, he walks up to the front door and knocks on it. The door opens, and a tall, sweaty bodybuilder stands there.

> MALTEX
> Hi. I'm looking for
> Laurencio Shivers.

> SHIVERS
> Yeah?

Maltex is taken back by Shivers' voice, it's deep and gravelly, like Harvey Fierstein's.

> MALTEX
> Are you him?

> SHIVERS
> Who are you?

He takes a deep drag from a cigarette.

> MALTEX
> Maltex Faloon. I'm following
> up on a donor fraud report
> you filed.

> SHIVERS
> Yeah. ...that was a while
> ago.

                    MALTEX
          Well, I'm investigating a
          whole list of cases. I was
          wondering if you could
          answer some questions.

                    SHIVERS
          I could have answered them
          a while ago.
                    (pause)
          Come in.

Maltex steps inside, through a cloud of
cigarette smoke.

INT. HOUSE

Maltex stands in the living room of the
strangely masculinely and femininely
decorated house. There are framed posters
of Mr. Shivers hanging on the walls. He's
some sort of bodybuilder drag queen.

                    SHIVERS
          Sit down.

                    MALTEX
          I'm sorry to dredge up old
          stuff. I'm sure some of
          this will be redundant——

                    SHIVERS
                    (interrupting)
          None of it will be
          redundant. You're the first
          one to show up about my
          report.

                    MALTEX
          Really?

                    SHIVERS
          Yes, really.

                    MALTEX
          I'm...sorry to hear that.
                    (pause)
          You contracted for a new
          voice? Is that right?

Shivers goes back to working out and
smoking, doing curls with two dumbbells. He
doesn't strain much to speak.

                    SHIVERS
          Yeah. I want a sexier
          voice.

He drops the dumbbells and starts posing
in front of a standing mirror. He points
out his figure.

                    SHIVERS
          I want to be more
          glamorous, see?

Maltex watches quietly.

                    SHIVERS
          Right now I sound like a
          Neanderthal.

Maltex stifles a comment.

Shivers is staring at the image in the
mirror. He flexes his pecks and arms
suddenly. His muscles rip impressively.

                    SHIVERS
          It's the one thing in the
          way of my being perfect.

He strikes another pose. Then another. He
seems upset by the thought.

Suddenly he looks at Maltex in the
reflection.

                    SHIVERS
          So what are you going to

do for me?

                    MALTEX
          Well, I'm trying to locate
          the man who defrauded you.

                    SHIVERS
          Twenty grand.

                    MALTEX
          Excuse me?

                    SHIVERS
          That's how much he took.

Maltex pauses, daydreaming about that
amount.

                    MALTEX
          That's a lot.

                    SHIVERS
          That's nothing. He said
          he had a line on a female
          voice box. It would have
          worked perfectly. What are
          my chances of getting a
          voice?

                    MALTEX
          Well, they're not good.

Maltex shuffles the folder in his lap.
Shivers notices his mittens.

                    MALTEX
          Could you describe him——

                    SHIVERS
                (interrupting)
          What's wrong with your
          hands?

This catches Maltex by surprise.

                    MALTEX
          It's not important.

                    SHIVERS
          How are you supposed to
          get this guy if you can't
          even get your mits off?

Maltex looks at Shivers. Shivers has a
clear look of disgust on his face.

                    MALTEX
          I'm not going to apprehend
          him. I'm just building the
          case against him.

                    SHIVERS
          What good will that do?

He steps toward Maltex.

                    MALTEX
          If I can cross reference
          how you came in contact
          with him, we can probably
          catch him.

                    SHIVERS
          Who's "we"? You're the only
          one who's responded to my
          report in... What...four
          months?

                    MALTEX
          All donor fraud cases are
          very——

                    SHIVERS
                (interrupting)
          If that folder there
          represents one person, he's
          been busy. What happens if
          you do find him?

                    MALTEX
          Usually, what happens is——

                    SHIVERS
                 (interrupting)
          He gets divided by the
          Jurisdiction, which is
          first-come, first-served.
          HMO will come first. Then
          whoever's next. Which means
          my chances are about zero.

He takes another step closer. Maltex stands
up.

                    MALTEX
          Look, I'm sorry about your
          situation, but if you help
          me out, you'd be doing
          yourself as well as all the
          other victims some good——

                    SHIVERS
                 (interrupting)
          What'd you call me?

Shivers grabs Maltex by the neck and spits
the cigarette out.

                    SHIVERS
          I'm not a victim, Mr.
          Cripple. Maybe I should
          just take yours. I have a
          black box, you know.

He starts choking him with one hand.
Maltex hugs the folder to his chest as
Shivers drags him to the door.

Shivers pushes Maltex against the wall.

                    SHIVERS
          I'm sure not going to
          get anything out of your
          pathetic help.

                    MALTEX
          Stop, please.

Maltex tries pathetically with one hand, actually one finger, to pry Shivers grip off his neck. He's starting to turn red.

Shivers leans against him bodily, almost grinding against him, enjoying Maltex's predicament.

                    SHIVERS
          "Stop, please?" They got
          cripples helping victims
          now?

Suddenly Maltex brings his knee up hard between Shivers' legs.

Shivers doubles over, extending his arm while still holding onto Maltex's neck.

                    SHIVERS
          Son of a bitch——

Shivers throws a punch with his left arm at Maltex's head. Maltex sags about a foot letting Shivers punch the wall.

Maltex then kicks with the same leg, this time with more momentum.

Shivers collapses to the floor, letting go of Maltex.

Maltex hurries out of the house and away.

Shivers coughs and sputters doubled over on the floor.

EXT. STREET - NIGHT

Maltex has walked away from Shivers' house. He rubs his neck, trying to breathe normally again. There's an obvious mark on his neck. He looks back the way he came, disgusted and annoyed.

He sighs and then continues on, determined.

INT. PAWNSHOP

Maltex is in a rundown pawnshop. He is
standing next to shelves of transparent
containers holding different body parts.

He's staring at a male left arm. It's not
very toned or muscular. His gaze drops to
the hand at the end of the appendage.

Maltex's face distorts through the curved
glass of the container. The container hums
from the preservation equipment in its
base.

The proprietor, BENNY FILLBOY, is behind a
steel mesh screen completing a phone call.

                    BENNY
          Twenty-five.
                    (pause)
          Alright, alright, jeez,
          fifteen. Yeah, okay. Bye.

He hangs up annoyed and comes out from
behind the screen.

                    BENNY
          Maltex!

Maltex pulls himself away from the arm in
the container.

                    MALTEX
          How you doin', Benny?

                    BENNY
          What I wouldn't give for
          some of the stuff I used
          to get.

                    MALTEX
          Yeah, tell me about it.

                    BENNY
          And you?

                    MALTEX
          I need a Flattener.

He frowns and then notices the bruise on
Maltex's neck.

                    BENNY
          You all right?

                    MALTEX
          Nutcase I interviewed
          decided to take it out on
          me.

                    BENNY
          Fuck. What happened?

                    MALTEX
          Kicked him in the nuts. Got
          outta' there.

Benny glances at Maltex's mittens.

                    BENNY
          How are your hands?

Maltex squints at him.

                    MALTEX
          They suck, Benny. I can't
          do shit. I'm getting tired
          of it.

Benny nods in pity.

                    MALTEX
          But,...I'm broke. I can't
          afford, I mean, I can't buy
          it from you.

Benny frowns slightly.

                    MALTEX
          Can you loan me one?

Benny can see that Maltex is upset. He
smiles at him.

                    BENNY
          No problem.

He goes behind the counter and from a
drawer pulls a small blue cylinder with two
prongs sticking out one end and a switch
on the side. He comes back out from behind
the counter and hands it to Maltex.

                    BENNY
          It's cold. No numbers.

Maltex nods and inspects it. He flicks the
switch once. A low HUM fills the air. Benny
ducks out of the way.

                    BENNY
          Watch where you point that.
          I like my engrams.

Maltex hits the switch again and the
HUM stops. As with anything, Maltex has
difficulty handling the device.

                    BENNY
          That should help.

                    MALTEX
          I won't tell you how I use
          it.

INT. PHONE CUBICLE

Maltex is checking his phone messages.

INSERT:
11:56 - DISCOVER CARD MONEY SERVICES -
AUDIO
05:34 - WALTHAM STREET PHARMACY - AUDIO
06:04 - FLEXIBEE BOLD - 4354355

Maltex clicks on WALTHAM STREET PHARMACY -
AUDIO.

                    RECORDING
          Uh, hi. Mr. Faloon? This is

                    Waltham Pharmacy calling
                    about an order you placed
                    for a refill on your
                    T-Butoxilina prescription.
                    Well, your credit card
                    denied the amount in
                    question--

Maltex deletes the message and drops his
head with a sigh. Maltex clicks on Flex's
number.

                         FLEX
                    (filtered)
          Hello?

Maltex winces when Flex speaks.

                         MALTEX
          It's Maltex. Maltex Faloon?
          You called?

                         FLEX
                    (hesitant)
          Yes. I did.

                         MALTEX
          Did you remember something
          more?

Maltex acts impatient. He types in a print
command and starts printing out more scans
from the file. He checks his watch.

                         FLEX
                    (filtered)
          Not exactly... I just
          thought we could talk.

                         MALTEX
          Talk?

                         FLEX
                    (filtered)
          I'm sure you're very busy.
          It's just that...

Maltex listens, expectantly. The printouts
slide out one by one.

                    FLEX
                 (filtered)
          Well, it's just that I
          don't usually talk much to
          anyone.
                 (pause)
          It's not every day I meet
          someone I can talk to
          about my...
                 (pause)
          My voice.

Maltex shifts his weight.

                    FLEX
                 (filtered)
          Know what I mean?

                    MALTEX
          Yes. I believe so.

                    FLEX
                 (filtered)
          I realized the other day
          that your hands are not...

Maltex is uncomfortable.

                    MALTEX
          That's true.

                    FLEX
                 (filtered)
          It's rare to find someone
          who seems to <u>understand</u>.
          You're very understanding,
          Mr. Faloon.

Maltex nods in recognition.

                    FLEX
                 (filtered)
          You listen like you've been
          there.

Maltex swallows and lets out a breath,
fidgets nervously.

                    FLEX
                 (filtered)
          Could we meet somewhere...
          and talk?

That startles Maltex.

INT. AUTOMAT

Maltex is sitting at a table in a cafe
with people sitting at internet terminals
scattered throughout. The foot traffic
offers Maltex some privacy.

He leafs through the new printout in the
file. He takes time with each one. He has
the folder propped in between his stomach
and the table.

With one hand he holds the pages he's
looked at, with the other he holds the
scan he's looking at, about to flip past
it. The next scan in order looks like
a scan of two hands, outstretched on a
scanner...

Flex walks in.

Maltex glances up at her and does a
double-take.

Flex is dressed in a green wraparound
leotard and a rust skirt that accentuates
her coloring and figure. She drapes her
raincoat on the back of the chair.

                    MALTEX
          You're here!?!

She smiles and looks around coyly.

                    MALTEX
          Would you like something?

She nods. Maltex gets up and they walk
over to the counter.

COUNTER

The server notices Flex's figure.

                    SERVER
          WhatcanIgetcha?

                    FLEX
               (hesitantly)
          Latte.

The server is taken back by her squawk.
Flex looks away.

                    SERVER
          Would you like a single or
          a double?

                    FLEX
               (hesitantly)
          Double.

Maltex watches quietly.

                    SERVER
          Foam? Vanilla? Sprinkles?

Flex sighs. Maltex notices her discomfort——

                    MALTEX
          Make it two regular
          Doubles. And a slice of——

He looks at Flex for corroboration as he
points out a plate in the display counter.
She nods.

                    MALTEX
          ——and a slice of carrot

            cake.

                    SERVER
            Okay.

Flex smiles at him.

The server places the items on the
counter. Maltex hands over some money and
leaves the change to the server's approval.

Maltex attempts to pick up the drinks and
the cake but Flex sweeps them up and leads
the way to their table.

She looks back at Maltex standing at the
counter. She nods at the table and smiles.
He joins her at the table.

                    FLEX
            Thank you.

                    MALTEX
            Thank you.

Flex sets the latte in front of him.

                              DISSOLVE TO:

Maltex and Flex are in deep discussion.

                    MALTEX
            The money could be better,
            but I don't have to do any
            rough stuff.
                    (pause)
            What about you?

                    FLEX
            Insurance office. Processing
            cases. Conforming data. Been
            there a while.

                    MALTEX
            You like it?

                    FLEX
          Not really. Like you said,
          it could be worse.

Maltex gazes at her. He stares at her eyes.
She smiles slightly. He gazes at her lovely
hands, holding her cup.

                    MALTEX
          How'd you wind up there?

                    FLEX
          Thought it might help me
          get a voice.

                    MALTEX
          Has it?

                    FLEX
          No. I'm just closer to the
          red tape.

She sighs audibly. It flutters slightly
through her artificial voice box.

                    MALTEX
          I'm sorry to hear that.

Flex leans forward, kind of hugging
herself. She smiles gratefully.

                    FLEX
          Thank you.

Maltex stares at her and takes a breath.

                    MALTEX
          I think you're _very_
          attractive.

He smiles, relieved, having said what was
distracting him.

Flex smiles even brighter, blushes. She
plays with her hair, brushes it off her
face.

                    FLEX
          How is the case going?

Grateful for the change of subject...

                    MALTEX
          This guy doesn't want to be
          found and it's very easy to
          hide.
                    (pause)
          If I learn enough, I might
          be able to lure him out of
          the dark. I.D. him and call
          the cops in.

                    FLEX
          How?

                    MALTEX
          Put an ad in the paper,
          posing as a possible mark.

                    FLEX
          And then?

                    MALTEX
          Try to locate him. I'd have
          to time it right.

                    FLEX
          Have you caught anyone
          before?

Maltex nods.

                    MALTEX
          Couple times. One guy was
          greedy and stupid. I put
          seven ads in the paper. He
          called all of them.
                    (pause)
          Another one skunked his
          neighbor, pissing in his
          own pool, as they say.

Flex chuckles. Maltex laughs quietly,

shaking his head.

> **FLEX**
> Then what would you do?

> **MALTEX**
> I've got to <u>build</u> a <u>case</u>.
> Connect the <u>dots</u> so HMO
> can section him out.
> (pause)
> Prove that that <u>specific</u>
> person defrauded these
> <u>specific</u> victims... A couple
> of my witnesses never saw
> him. One met him, but
> doesn't remember what he
> looks like.

Maltex hisses an exasperated breath out,
shaking his head.

> **FLEX**
> What?

> **MALTEX**
> This odd geezer wanted to
> buy my leg. Got to where
> I was trying to get away
> from him, actually dragging
> him <u>hanging</u> off my leg.

> **FLEX**
> Really?

> **MALTEX**
> Yeah. And this drag queen
> today almost choked the
> life out of me.

> **FLEX**
> What?

> **MALTEX**
> This psycho threatened to
> take my voice box. I guess
> he was just frustrated.

                    FLEX
          Your voice?

                     MALTEX
          He wants a female voice
          or something to finish
          his work of art, his body.
          Even said he has a black
          surgical box.

Maltex shrugs. Flex reaches across the
table and caresses Maltex's right mitten.

                    FLEX
          I didn't realize.

Maltex looks up at her and smiles. He
gazes at her longingly.

                    MALTEX
          You want to get out of
          here?

Flex sparkles at the thought.

                    FLEX
          Sure.

They get up.

EXT. STREET

Flex and Maltex are walking casually down
the street. Maltex has the ubiquitous file
under his arm. Flex has her hands in her
coat pockets.

                    FLEX
          My mother and my father
          were working at the plants
          they had down in Tennessee
          when she had me. The ones
          HMO shut down.
                    (pause)
          It hit my larynx when I

                    was twenty. Just as my
                    singing was taking off. It
                    just started falling apart.

Maltex winces a bit.

                         FLEX
                    The good news is that it
                    tends to hit you once.
                    It probably won't spread.
                    Still...

Maltex and Flex come to an apartment
building.

                         MALTEX
                    This is my place.

She looks at the building.

                         MALTEX
                    Would you like to come up?

She looks at Maltex.

                         FLEX
                    Sure. I'd like that.

Maltex opens the front door and allows
Flex in.

INT. MALTEX'S APARTMENT

Flex is sitting on Maltex's sofa/bed. She
looks around the cluttered apartment.
Maltex comes in from the kitchen carrying
two tumblers clutched between his mittens.

                         FLEX
                    Need help?

                         MALTEX
                    I'm okay.

Maltex carries the drinks to the coffee
table. He shoves a pile aside to clear a

space and sets them down.

                    MALTEX
          Scotch, soda.

Flex takes a sip of her drink.

                    MALTEX
          I'd been playing pool since
          I was ten.
                    (pauses)
          Professional, unbeatable.

Maltex cups his drink in one hand and
supports the side with the other. He holds
it up to his mouth and drinks. Even that
is painful to his hands. He sits back and
sighs.

                    MALTEX
          Anyway, I was just
          practicing in a pool hall
          when this guy comes up and
          pitches a game.

He looks like a granny holding his drink
on his stomach. He notices and becomes
self-conscious. He takes another drink and
sets it down on the table.

                    MALTEX
          After the first game he
          suggested a small wager.
          We played for hours,
          game after game. He made
          stupid mistakes, going for
          the wrong shot, hitting
          something a touch too hard.
          I won each game.

Maltex pauses and looks at his hands.

                    MALTEX
          I let him out of it a
          bunch of times but he
          insisted on playing.

                    Gradually I lost interest.
                              (pauses)
                    And then I lost.

Maltex looks away. Flex does a double take,
she perks up.

                         FLEX
                    What? What do you mean?

                         MALTEX
                    He had set me up
                    beautifully. It was double
                    or nothing. I was ahead,
                    and I lost.

Maltex looks at her. His eyes are bright,
embarrassed.

                         MALTEX
                    That surprised me. I didn't
                    have money, I had won it
                    all from him. So I wanted
                    another game.

He reaches for his drink again, gulps some
down.

                         MALTEX
                    He wanted collateral.

                         FLEX
                    Your hands?

Maltex raises the tumbler in both hands
almost like an offering. He looks at his
deformed hands clutching the glass.

                         MALTEX
                    When that last game was
                    over, I'd lost.

                         FLEX
                    What do you mean?

                    MALTEX
          He'd taken my hands. Gone.
                    (pause)
          They'd been removed with
          transplant boxes. At first
          I thought he'd done it
          because of the money. Then
          I figured it was his idea
          from the start.

                    FLEX
          What did you do then?

                    MALTEX
          Stumbled to a hospital and
          got these welfares.

                    FLEX
          Why didn't you buy a decent
          set? You must've had money
          from competing.

                    MALTEX
          I was _stunned_. I was
          depressed. How could I have
          been suckered so easily?
          I drank my money away.
          By the time I came up
          for breath, my hands had
          already started to go.

Maltex stares at his aged and damaged
hands.

Flex gets closer to Maltex and takes his
hand, gently, in hers. Maltex looks up from
his hands and looks into her eyes.

There are tears in his eyes.

                    MALTEX
          That really hurts.

Flex looks down at her hand rubbing his,
and pulls her hand away.

                    FLEX
          Sorry.

Maltex leans forward and kisses her. She
kisses him back.

They both kiss, becoming more passionate.

Maltex tries to undo her top but is
hampered by his mittens. He slips them off
but becomes self-conscious again.

She looks at his hands and then at him and
kisses him. She guides his hands to her
top. He still has difficulty, and pain.

                    FLEX
          It's okay.

Flex takes his hands in hers and gently
kisses them.

Then she slowly, tantalizingly, unfastens
her top revealing her full breasts.

She guides his curled fingers to caress
a breast. He tries to caress her but his
hands make it futile, ridiculous. The
frustration builds inside him, embarrassing
him.

He collapses into her shoulder.

                    MALTEX
          I can't do anything with
          these. I can't even make
          love to you.

He turns away to stand up but Flex stops
him. She pulls him back down.

Flex kisses him and then pushes him onto
his back. She climbs on top, pinning him.

INT. BEDROOM - MORNING

Maltex is awake, lying in his bed. Flex is sleeping with her head on his chest. Her right hand is holding his left wrist. He's gazing at her beautiful hand.

                    FLEX
          Maltex?

Maltex is surprised to hear she's awake.

                    MALTEX
          Yeah?

                    FLEX
What are my chances...of getting a voice?

                    MALTEX
          They're...not good.

                    FLEX
          If I had money?

                    MALTEX
          You'd still be on a list.

She's quiet for a while, then.

                    FLEX
          What about his?

                    MALTEX
          Whose?

                    FLEX
          Turgidson. What about his?

She lifts herself up to look at him and kisses him.

                    FLEX (CONT'D)
          He's a criminal, a crook.
          He's going to get split up
          and given away.

84

                    MALTEX
          Yeah?

                    FLEX
          But what if we find him?

Maltex looks at her doubtfully.

                    FLEX (CONT'D)
          We knock him out, take his
          larynx.

                    MALTEX
          What?

She caresses his left hand and kisses it.

                    FLEX
          And his hands.

Maltex laughs.

                    MALTEX
          And leave him dead?

                    FLEX
          Not necessarily.

Maltex thinks it's ridiculous but continues
thinking.

                    FLEX (CONT'D)
          I'm sure you could figure
          out some way. You seem
          to have handled yourself
          pretty well with that
          bodybuilding drag queen.

                    MALTEX
          I can't do that. I need to
          get paid. I, I,...

                    FLEX
          Oh come on. What do you
          want in life?

Flex sits up naked exhibiting her gorgeous body.

                    FLEX (CONT'D)
          Quit the case. We'll find
          him on our own.

Maltex glances at her eyes and then her breasts, and then back at her eyes.

                    FLEX (CONT'D)
          The department won't help
          you. They don't give a shit
          about you.

                    MALTEX
          That's a whole world of
          trouble--

                    FLEX
               (interrupting)
          Nobody will care. I see how
          the insurance companies
          deal with it. They cut
          any corner they need to.
          Do you think anyone cares
          what happens to a stinking
          low-life DF?

She huddles closer to him forcing him to sit up in bed.

                    FLEX (CONT'D)
          Think about it, Baby. The
          cops have better things to
          do.

She can see that Maltex sees her point. She lets him think about it for a moment. Then...

She arches her back slightly raising her breasts.

                    FLEX (CONT'D)
          What would you give for a

<u>new</u> set of <u>hands</u>?

Maltex can't argue with her. She smiles
when she sees that her point hits home.

Maltex gazes at Flex longingly. She looks
like a 1950s paperback moll.

Frustratedly, he shakes his head and gets
out of bed.

> MALTEX
> I don't know, Flex. I--

Flex looks disappointed suddenly. She
watches him go into the bathroom. He
starts the shower and closes the door.

She slumps down frustrated, frowning,
crossing her arms.

INT. SHOWER

Maltex is pumping shampoo from a bottle
onto the heels of his hands. He starts
lathering his hair with his fists.

Next he tries to grab a bar of soap. He
has obvious practice, but it's still a
daunting task to pick up slippery soap
with arthritic hands.

The bar of soap shoots out of his grip. He
chases it around the tub.

INT. BEDROOM

Flex looks on the nightstand and sees
Maltex's assorted TV remotes. She picks up
a remote and turns on the television.

She can hear the BANGING of the elusive
bar of soap on the tub.

She finds another remote and turns on
the VCR. It's a tape of a pool game in a

tournament. She recognizes a young Maltex playing. She smiles and pauses it on a close-up of Maltex, to make sure.

INT. SHOWER

Maltex corners the bar of soap against the porcelain and raises it to a level where it drops in his palms, or what there is of his palms.

He starts lathering his chest when the soap scoots away from him again.

                    MALTEX
          Goddamnit.

Maltex sighs long and hard and leans against the tile wall, under the shower, thinking.

INT. BEDROOM

Flex gets off the bed, and sits close to the screen, examining the image.

In the shot she also notices Maltex's hands on his cue stick. Though the image is fuzzy and grainy, it is clear that on the back of Maltex's hand is a tattoo identical to Blass's tattoo.

She hears Maltex cursing and banging around in the bathroom.

She hits the fast forward button and finds another vantage point of the tattoo confirming it for herself.

She hears the shower shut off and Maltex climb out. She hits the play button.

Maltex comes out and glances at the screen and at Flex.

                    MALTEX
          You discovered my past.

Flex smiles slightly and nods.

                    FLEX
          Yeah. You look good.

She looks at him as if asking a question,
"Well?"

                    MALTEX
          I need to do some work.

Flex and he just stare at each other for
a moment. He starts dressing avoiding the
subject.

She just watches him quietly, as he
struggles to get dressed. He stops in mid
struggle with some buttons and looks at
her.

                    MALTEX
          I've got to...check some
          stuff out before...

Flex smiles slightly. Maltex pulls his
perennially looped tie over his head and
starts for the door.

                    MALTEX
          I'll be back in a little
          while.

Maltex pauses with his hand on the
doorknob. He looks at her then opens the
door and leaves.

Flex gets out of bed to collect her
clothes. She stops and thinks for a
moment. She turns and looks at the door.

She gets dressed moving about the
apartment.

Grabbing her coat she notices a shelf

cluttered full against a wall. She notices that Maltex has two BLACK BOXES in their cases.

Waiting.

INT. BOVINE WOMAN'S HOUSE - DAY

Maltex stands facing an obese woman PHYLLIS and her husband, PHIL, in what used to be a marble floored living room, now dominated by a round bed surrounded by contraptions. He's holding the case folder open.

The Bovine woman is in bed connected to eight hoses that lead to a big espresso-like machine, with a golden eagle on top, that chugs laboriously. The woman grunts while gnawing on fried chicken.

Phil tends to the espresso-like waste processing machine.

                    MALTEX
          How long had the ad been
          in that paper before he
          contacted you?

                    PHIL
          Two days. I knew he would
          do this.
                    (to his wife)
          Didn't I say we couldn't
          trust him?

                    PHYLLIS
          You never said anything.
          You never know what you're
          talking about.

                    PHIL
          I even asked him point
          blank if he was planning
          on cheating us.

Maltex chuckles and looks up surprised.

                    MALTEX
          Really? What did he say?

                    PHIL
          He assured us he was
          completely trustworthy.

                    PHYLLIS
          Of course he said that. Do
          you think he'd tell you if
          he was planning on ripping
          me off?

The little man glares at his wife, then
goes back to what he was doing.

                    MALTEX
          What did you contract for?

                    PHIL
          A stomach.

Maltex glances at the enormous woman.

                    MALTEX
          Is that a mechanical one?

The husband glances at the contraption and
then at Maltex.

                    PHIL
          Oh, no. That's a PRO-cessor.
          To help out. She has eight.

Maltex is confused.

                    MALTEX
          Eight? What?

                    PHIL
          Stomachs.

Maltex stares at the woman again. She
tosses a bone into a stainless steel bowl

and grabs another piece of chicken.

                    MALTEX
                  (shocked)
          What?

                    PHYLLIS
          To eat more.

Maltex looks at her. She stops eating for
a moment and pulls herself up, as much as
she can.

                    PHYLLIS
          I love to eat.

Maltex can't believe the situation. He
looks at Phil.

                    MALTEX
          You mean she doesn't need a
          stomach?

                    PHIL
          Need?

                    PHYLLIS
          Of course I need one.
          These aren't enough.

                    PHIL
          She eats _more than_ the
          eight can handle.

Phil smiles at Maltex as if that
information were cute. Maltex looks
shocked.

                    MALTEX
          How...much...did you pay
          him?

                    PHIL
          Only twenty-seven five.
          Fifty percent. HMO gets at
          least seventy thousand.

Maltex is suddenly pale and looks at them
as if they're insane.

                    MALTEX
          Twenty-seven thousand, five
          hundred?

                    PHIL
          I wanted to do a real
          credit check, but she was
          in a hurry...

                    PHYLLIS
          Shutup. It was beautiful.
          Someone else would get it.

The husband looks at Maltex, then at his
wife.

                    PHIL
          Maybe now you'll listen to
          me, Darling.

Phil looks back at Maltex, conspiratorially.

                    PHIL
          This is the second time.

The Bovine woman erupts from her eating
with a shout.

                    PHYLLIS
          Stop chattering over there.
          Phil, get something done,
          Jesus Christ.

                    MALTEX
          The second time?

                    PHIL
          Someone else defrauded us
          on an esophagus Phyllis
          wanted.

                    PHYLLIS
          Shutup.

                    PHIL
                 (whispered)
          It was a while ago.

After a moment, although flabbergasted,
Maltex fishes out scans and hands them to
Phil. It hurts to do so.

                   MALTEX
          Does this look like it?

The woman becomes agitated.

                   PHYLLIS
          Gimme, gimme.

                    PHIL
          Hold on, Phyllis.

Phil walks over to her looking at the
scans and hands them to her one by one. He
holds the stamped one up to Maltex.

                    PHIL
          This is the one he gave
          us. See it has an insurance
          stamp on it. That's not
          supposed to be possible,
          is it? I mean it's a real
          stamp, right?

INSERT:
Medical scans. One of them has a
rubberstamped logo, FRYE & COOKE Ins. Reg.
Authority-#11639A66548. 03:47

Maltex notices the stamp and focuses on it.

She grabs the scans with her greasy hands
and stares longingly at them, caressing
them.

                   PHYLLIS
          It's so pretty.

She flips through the different scans.

                    PHYLLIS
          They're the same.

                    MALTEX
          Are you sure?

                    PHYLLIS
          It's so beautiful...

She starts to get weepy. Maltex looks at
Phil.

                    MALTEX
          What does he look like?

Phil stops moving about and thinks for a
moment.

                    PHIL
          I don't know. Uh, just...
          average I suppose.

Maltex holds the folder open to Phil.

                    MALTEX
          I'm trying to put together
          a facsimile of his face.
          Does this look like him?

Maltex holds up the patchwork he's made of
the different scans taped together.

                    PHIL
          No, I don't recognize
          these.

                    MALTEX
          Look closely.

                    PHIL
          Those are the only ones
          I recognize. Isn't that
          enough?

                    MALTEX
          What about this?

He points at the nose. The man shakes his head. Maltex points at the ears.

> MALTEX
> This?

The man shakes his head again.

> PHIL
> I didn't really pay
> attention to the man
> himself.

> MALTEX
> I _need_ to have some cross-
> referencing. Maybe your
> wife would recognize some
> of the other...

They look at Phyllis. She's weeping and eating while staring at the scans in her hand. Maltex stops short. Then he steps forward and grabs the pictures from her. She shrieks at him.

> PHYLLIS
> Phil??

> PHIL
> It's alright, Darling.

Annoyed, Maltex tries to wipe grease off the scans and return them to the folder. He fumbles and drops the folder. The scans slide all over the marble floor.

> PHIL
> It's alright. We'll find you
> another stomach.
> (to Maltex)
> What's wrong with you?
> Grabby!

Maltex is on his knees trying to collect the scans. He stops at a scan of hands; backsides.

                    PHIL
          Who taught you manners?

Maltex doesn't respond. He stares at the
scan, mindlessly gathering the rest to his
chest.

                    PHIL
          What is it?

Maltex is still quiet.

INSERT:
Maltex is staring at a tattoo, in the scan,
between the thumb and index finger, the
same as the one Blass has.

Maltex stares at it, his mouth hanging
open.

Finally, he stands. He turns to leave. Phil
grabs his shoulder.

                    PHIL
          Hey! What's going on? Is
          that it?

Maltex looks at him blankly. He starts to
open the door.

                    PHIL
          Where you going?

Maltex leaves.

INT. BATHROOM STALL

Maltex is sitting on a closed toilet, not
using it.

He's staring at the scan of the hands with
a mad look on his face. In a neighboring
stall someone is groaning loudly.

Maltex stares at the image and then at
his hands in his mittens, holding them up

dejectedly.

He rummages through the folder again and finds the scan of the stomach with the FRYE & COOKE stamp. He thinks about it.

Finally he buries his head in his arms.

INT. PHONE CUBICLE

Maltex dials up the bounty files. He types in his I.D. number.

In a corner of the screen an alert appears directing Maltex to type in his case authorization code. Numbers begin counting down from thirty.

Maltex types in his code and starts accessing files. He types in a request. A new screen appears.

INSERT:
New reports: Complainant: Lane, Molly, prostitute; address...

Maltex prints out that information. He then types in another request.

INSERT:
Researching Medical Scan Authorization; FRYE & COOKE Ins. Reg. Authority-#11639A66548. 03:47

Maltex types in another request.

INSERT:
Insurance agent: Bold, Flexibee

Maltex sits back and stares at the screen. Maltex goes offline and leaves the cubicle with his new printouts.

INT. HALLWAY

Maltex walks along until he finds a door.

He knocks. Waits and knocks again.

                    MOLLY
               (through door)
          Yeah?

                    MALTEX
          My name's Faloon. You
          registered a Donor Fraud
          complaint?

The door opens slowly. MOLLY stands there,
slightly shielded by the door, wearing a
tattered bathrobe.

Maltex pulls out the image of the hands.

                    MALTEX
          Do you recognize this?

Molly takes the picture and stares at it.
She nods and hands it back.

                    MOLLY
          Yeah, that's his. That
          shithead. Did you find him?

                    MALTEX
          Could you describe him?

Molly stands back and opens the door
wider. Maltex goes in.

INT. HOTEL ROOM

Molly crosses to the bed and sits. She
retrieves a cigarette from a pack on the
bed and lights it. Her neck and chest is
more wrinkly than her face. Her right arm
is darker than her left...

Maltex closes the door. Molly takes a drag.

                    MOLLY
          It's not likely I'm going to
          forget that fuck's face for

a while.

                    MALTEX
          Yeah?

                    MOLLY
          He said he could get me a
          complete set--

                    MALTEX
               (interrupting)
          What's he look like?

                    MOLLY
          About your size. Average
          looking, dark hair. And
          that thing.

She points at the tattoo on the scan.

                    MALTEX
          How did he contact you?

                    MOLLY
          At a poolhall, Ace's--

At that Maltex leans forward.

                    MALTEX
               (nearly whispering)
          He was playing pool? Was he
          good?

                    MOLLY
               (confused)
          Yeah, you could say that.
          He took one of the crows
          down for a lot of cash.

Maltex exhales as though he has been
holding his breath for a long time. He
turns and leaves.

                    MOLLY
          Hey. Where you going? Hey?

INT. FLEX'S OFFICE

Flex is sitting at her desk. She types commands into her terminal.

INSERT:
CASE NO. 83227-004 –– Faloon, Maltex;
Ident. 640FIWT-DZ-282.
Column authority, class-B.

ASSIGNMENT STATUS: UP TO DATE

She frowns looking at the screen. Then she slips on her headset and dials from her keyboard.

EXT. ACE'S POOLHALL

As Maltex approaches the poolhall two young, stupid-looking men rush up to him and drag him struggling off into the alley next-door. One of them has a bandage on his nose, it's the Punk who jumped Maltex in the alley.

The Punk pushes him against the wall about to throw a punch. Maltex focuses on him and they both recognize each other.

                    PUNK
          Wait a second.

Maltex throws an elbow at him but he sidesteps.

                    PUNK
          Watch out for this guy,
          Rob. He's dangerous.

                    MAN #2
          Shut up.

They throw Maltex about, bouncing him off the walls and garbage cans. Maltex falls and the folder scatters on the ground.

The Punk bends down and grabs one of Maltex's hands. He squeezes slowly. Maltex desperately tries to break free. With his other hand he pulls out the <u>flattener</u>. He points it at the Punk.

The Punk stops and looks blankly down at Maltex. Maltex fires. The Punk is suddenly compressed from front to back, flattened, and then he pops back into shape. He lets out a gasp and drops to the ground hard.

Man #2 starts to run away. Maltex aims and fires. Man #2 gasps as he too gets flattened and then drops.

Maltex sits up and shakily gropes for the vial of T-Butoxilina and the syringe. He finally injects himself through the mitten.

The pain slowly recedes. He sits there in the filth, thinking. He clutches the flattener.

He gets up slowly and goes to one of the torpid men. He pats the Punk down, searching his pockets.

From one of the pockets Maltex pulls out a Polaroid. He holds it up and looks at it.

INSERT:
It's a photo of Maltex standing at a front door, taken by a surveillance camera.

FLASHBACK: Maltex is waiting on the stoop of Flexibee's brownstone as she opens the door and greets him.

End of FLASHBACK

Maltex frowns and wags the Polaroid, not knowing what to do with it, but with a new understanding of the situation.

INT. MALTEX'S APARTMENT/FLEX'S OFFICE,

INTERCUT

Maltex is drying his face with a towel.
He's cradling his phone in his shoulder. He
looks tense.

                    MALTEX
          Hi. It's me.

                    FLEX
               (filtered)
          Hey. Where are you?

                    MALTEX
          Home.

FLEX'S OFFICE

                    FLEX
          Did I lock your door right?

                    MALTEX
               (filtered)
          Yeah, no problem. Hey,
          is there anything else
          you can tell me about
          this guy? Anything you
          remember?

                    FLEX
          Like what?

                    MALTEX
               (filtered)
          Did he ever call you at
          work?

Flex thinks for a moment.

                    FLEX
          No, just my classified ad
          voicemail.

                    MALTEX
               (filtered)
          What about his name? Did

he ever mention the name
<u>Blass Grix</u>?

Flex is momentarily stopped. She tries to
hide her surprise.

                    FLEX
          Like I said in my report,
          he said his name was
          Turgidson. I figured he
          didn't want to use his real
          name.

MALTEX'S APARTMENT

                    MALTEX
          Hhhm. Okay.

                    FLEX
               (filtered)
          Good. Did you think about
          what we talked about?

                    MALTEX
          Yeah, I'm not sure it's a
          good idea.

FLEX'S OFFICE

                    FLEX
          Don't you want new hands?

                    MALTEX
               (filtered)
          Yes, but.

                    FLEX
          We can both win in this.

                    MALTEX
               (filtered)
          If he doesn't want to get
          ferreted out...

                    FLEX
          What about those ads you

placed?

                    MALTEX
                  (filtered)
          Well, he'll either call...or
          not.

                    FLEX
          Try to be a little
          positive.

MALTEX'S APARTMENT

                    MALTEX
          I'm not a cowboy. I'm not
          about to start acting like
          one.

                    FLEX
                  (filtered)
          I see.

                    MALTEX
          Well, you would if you'd
          just been jumped by two
          guys who were obviously
          sent after you...

Maltex hangs up.

FLEX'S OFFICE

Flex dials a phone number.

                    BLASS
                  (filtered)
          Hello?

                    FLEX
          He found out who you are.

                    BLASS
                  (filtered)
          How?

                    FLEX
          I don't know how. But then
          I think you know him too.

INT. HOTEL ROOM/FLEX'S OFFICE, INTERCUT

                    FLEX
                 (filtered)
          Something about you
          hustling him in a pool
          game once.

Blass holds up his right hand, looks at
the tattoo between the thumb and index
finger. He opens and closes his hand.

There's a slight scar that circles his
wrist.

                    BLASS
          I have to get out of here.

                    FLEX
                 (filtered)
          What about my voice?

                    BLASS
          That's going to have to
          wait.

FLEX'S OFFICE

Flex is desperately trying to persuade him.

                    FLEX
          I don't think he's going to
          let you go that easily.
                 (pause)
          I've got a better idea.

                    BLASS
                 (filtered)
          Yeah?

                    FLEX
          There's no telling where
          he's been, what trouble
          he's stirred up. Set up a
          meeting with him. Kill him.

                    BLASS
                 (filtered)
          Kill him? I already
          arranged for something like
          that.

                    FLEX
          It didn't work!

                    BLASS
                 (filtered)
          ...I suppose you have a
          point.

                    FLEX
          Have you seen his ads?

                    BLASS
                 (filtered)
          Yeah.

                    FLEX
          Good.

Flex hangs up and types some keys on her
keyboard. A screen pops up and she prints
that page.

She gets up and walks over to a big clunky
printer in the corner. She grabs the
printout.

INSERT:
Complainant name: SHIVERS, Laurencio
Address: 22319 Tower St.

Flex nods to herself emphatically.

INT. MALTEX'S APARTMENT

Maltex has the phone cradled in his
shoulder.

He walks over to his cluttered shelf and
picks up one of his black boxes in its
case. He blows dust off of it, opens the
case and takes out the black box. He flips
a switch on it, turning it on, checking
its functionality.

                    CABBIE
                  (filtered)
          Yeah?

                    MALTEX
          It's Maltex, Cabbie.

                    CABBIE
                  (filtered)
          Hey. What can I do for ya'?

                    MALTEX
          It's important. I need your
          help. Can you come pick me
          up?

                    CABBIE
                  (filtered)
          Sure, Maltex.

Maltex hangs up and dials another number.
He waits. He looks at the videotaped pool
game running on his television.

                    MALTEX
          Classifieds. Box 2234.

Maltex enters a code on his phone keypad.
An automated voice comes on the line.

                    AUTOMATED VOICE
          You - have - one - new -
          response - as - of - five
          - forty - one - press -

                    three - to - review.

Maltex looks at his clock, presses three
on the keypad. It's six o'clock.

                    BLASS
                   (filtered)
          I'm responding to the
          ad you placed for the
          mouthal appendage. I'm in
          possession of a very nice
          unit. I'm leaving town
          soon, possibly tomorrow,
          and I'm looking for a
          fast transaction. I've got
          a black box. If you're
          interested meet me at Hotel
          Utah, room four twenty-six,
          eight o'clock tonight. Let
          me know if you're coming -
          beep

Maltex listens to the voice and nods.
He sees himself as a younger pool shark
on the videotape. He pauses the tape on
a close-up, almost exactly as Flex did
earlier. He sees the tattoo on his right
hand in the freeze-frame.

He presses a button on the keypad.

                    MALTEX
          Thanks for your response.
          Yes, definitely very
          interested. I'd like to at
          least take a look at it
          and check the paperwork.
          I'll see you at eight as
          you said.

Maltex hangs up and then shuts off the
videotape of himself.

EXT. SHIVERS' HOUSE

Flex walks up the porch to the door. She
rings the bell. Shivers opens the door,
smoking and glares at her.

                    SHIVERS
          What do you want, sister?

Flex takes out a purple automatic pistol
from her coat pocket and points it at him.
In surprise he steps back.

INT. SHIVERS' HOUSE

Flex steps in and closes the door.

                    SHIVERS
          What, what do you want?

She notices his strange voice, grimaces.

                    FLEX
          You have a black box.

Shivers peers at her when he notices her
artificial voice.

                    FLEX
          Where?

He glances inadvertently to his right. Flex
notices.

                    SHIVERS
          I don't know what you're
          talking about.

Flex shoots him twice. He doubles over and
hits the floor.

She moves to the left where he glanced and
opens a bureau. Inside she finds a black
box designed for the neck area.

She steps over Shivers and looks at his

neck. She thinks for a moment.

                    SHIVERS
                  (gravelly)
              God—damn—you...

He has a horrible voice. She decides
against taking his voice and leaves.

INT. TAXICAB - EVENING

Cabbie opens the passenger door to let
Maltex in.

                    MALTEX
              Thanks a lot, Cabbie. You
              know I wouldn't ask you if
              it wasn't important. I'll
              pay you one way or another
              if this works out.

Cabbie looks at Maltex compassionately. He
seems to be thinking of all the reasons he
knows to pity Maltex.

                    CABBIE
              I hear ya'. So what's the
              action?

Maltex settles in, closes the door and
hands him a slip of paper. He places a
carpet bag on his lap.

                    MALTEX
              Let's go here.

Cabbie drives off, puffing on his pipe.

LATER

Maltex and Cabbie are parked across the
street, a short distance from Flexibee's
brownstone.

Maltex is slumped down in his seat,
staring across the street. Cabbie is

reading a newspaper.

                    MALTEX
          Have you paid off this cab
          yet?

                    CABBIE
          Hell no. But's it's my
          lease.

Flexibee comes out of her apartment,
carrying a backpack. Maltex perks up. She
looks around and gets into her old car.

                    MALTEX
          Here we go.

Cabbie catches on. He starts the engine
and pulls into traffic, careful to let
another car get between them.

                    CABBIE
          Alrighty.

EXT. HOTEL UTAH - NIGHT

Cabbie and Maltex slow down outside the
hotel as they watch Flex walk inside. This
is not the posh hotel Blass was staying at
before.

                    CABBIE
          Do we wait?

                    MALTEX
          Nah. You can take off.

Cabbie looks at him, surprised, then
concerned.

                    CABBIE
          Where you going?

                    MALTEX
          I'm not sure.

                    CABBIE
          Tell you what. I'll be out
          here.

Maltex starts to object but Cabbie's
expression tells him it's futile. He nods
at him appreciatively and gets out of the
cab with the carpet bag.

                    MALTEX
          Thanks, buddy.

                    CABBIE
          Watch yourself.

Maltex smiles, nods and then crosses the
street.

INT. HOTEL ROOM

Blass opens the door and let's Flex into
the dumpy room. She's tense, flexing her
jaw muscles. He seems nervous too.

                    BLASS
          What's so important about
          you being here?

He has a pistol on the table. He picks it
up, hefts it.

                    FLEX
          You're going to need help.
          How many people have you
          killed?

Blass thinks for a moment. He's not a
violent criminal, just a crook.

                    BLASS
          What? You're saying you
          have experience?

                    FLEX
          No. I just know it's not
          that simple. You learn

> things working in an
> insurance office.

He puts the pistol down uncertainly. He turns around rubbing his forehead.

> FLEX
> Also, I want to safeguard
> my interest.

Blass turns around, puzzled. Then patronizingly...

> BLASS
> You want to take his
> larynx?

She stares into his eyes.

> FLEX
> Blass, you don't have any
> intention of getting my
> larynx, do you? I'm another
> scam, aren't I? I've been
> useful to you. That's why
> you've strung me along all
> this time.

Blass is surprised by her. He becomes obsequious.

> BLASS
> You've got it wrong. That
> singer's voice I told you
> about. I'm working on it.
> Remember?

> FLEX
> I was just another scam,
> right?

> BLASS
> What are you talking about?

> FLEX
> I've seen the file. I've

                    been a convenience. Get
                    laid, keep tabs on your
                    pursuer. Pretty good deal,
                    huh?

Flex turns casually around and reaches
into her pocket. Blass watches her back.

                    BLASS
          You're being ridiculous. You
          don't know what you're——

Then Flex turns around, holding the purple
automatic.

Flex shoots him once in the chest. He
falls back gasping and rolls to one side
on the bed.

INT. HOTEL LOBBY

Maltex looks around the lobby. He makes
his way to the elevators. There are very
few people around, although it's a fairly
large hotel; it's just rundown.

He moves to the stairwell and starts
climbing, holding the carpet bag under one
arm.

INT. HALLWAY

Maltex emerges from the stairwell and
moves down the hall, checking room numbers
as he goes.

He finds the room. He leans against the
door and listens. There are some RUSTLING
noises. He quietly checks the door handle.
It's locked.

He reaches in his coat and takes out the
flattener.

He backs up against the wall, lunges

against the door and hits it with his shoulder. The door swings in and he enters.

INT. HOTEL ROOM

Maltex sees Blass's body propped against the headboard with a bullet wound in the chest and a bloody mess under the chin. He seems to be looking up suddenly at Maltex. Maltex points the flattener at Blass.

Suddenly, Flex comes from the side and hits Maltex's hand, knocking the flattener to the floor. He drops the carpet bag and clutches his hand in AGONY, as if he had stubbed a toe.

                    MALTEX
          Goddamnit...

She steps in front of Maltex and aims the pistol at him. She has Shivers' black box on her neck.

She blinks as it finishes its job. She flicks a switch off, releasing herself. She tosses the box on the bed.

Maltex stares at her, his expression clears.

                    MALTEX
               (breathlessly)
          What did you do?

Flex holds the gun on Maltex more confidently.

                    FLEX
          I came to get what's mine.

Her voice is that of <u>Blass</u> now, <u>not the mechanical voice</u>.

Flex looks at the carpet bag and the black

boxes that tumbled out. She recognizes
them as inappropriate for her task.

Maltex stares at her as she tries to
figure out her voice.

                    FLEX
             (clears her throat)
          ...And you seem to have
          come for what's yours.

Maltex looks at them himself.

                    MALTEX
          You took his larynx.

                    FLEX
          Just like you're gonna'
          take his hands. Or should
          I say your hands?

He looks at her.

                    MALTEX
          Insurance agency? Frye and
          Cooke? The authorization
          code on Blass's phony
          medicals was from "F/C
          Insurance."
             (pause)
          You've been working for him
          the whole time. You knew
          where he was. You were
          never a victim. You were
          just...keeping tabs on me.

Maltex shakes his head incredulously.

                    MALTEX (CONT'D)
          And I thought you cared
          about me.

                    FLEX
          I thought you cared about
          me, too. You really did
          seem to understand.

She coughs and rubs her throat with her
free hand.

                    FLEX (CONT'D)
          I've been trying to get
          my voice. I've tried
          everything, never content
          to leave it the way it is.
          I even started to think if
          I helped you, you'd help
          me.

She steps back.

                    FLEX (CONT'D)
          I felt sorry for you. But
          then I realized that's all
          you need to be content
          with yourself, for people
          to feel sorry for you.
          When I saw that you weren't
          going to do anything to
          improve your situation...
          just continue to sit and
          watch ancient videotapes of
          your past life. Well, I got
          tired of depending on men.

                    MALTEX
          I...

                    FLEX
          I don't see the box you
          brought for my voice
          anywhere.

Her finger tightens on the trigger. Maltex
throws his hands up in front of his face.

                    MALTEX
          No.

She shifts her aim and fires a hole into
the center of Blass' left hand. Then the
right. Maltex looks up, horrified to see
his hands destroyed.

He drops his hands, his mouth hanging open, staring at the ruin of his life.

Flex turns around again and aims at his head. Maltex looks at her in anguish.

                    MALTEX (CONT'D)
          Why?

Flex stares at him and shakes her head. She seems genuinely concerned.

                    FLEX
          What difference would that
          make?

Maltex's eyes widen.

                    FLEX (CONT'D)
          The question is, What are
          you going to do about it?

He glances at the gun and then back at her eyes.

His right arm shoots up into her jaw. His fist makes a loud WHACK against her chin. Her head snaps back and she drops like a sack.

His face twists in pain as his legs collapse, and he drops to the floor, nearly passing out. He writhes for a while as he cradles his hand with the other. Tears drop from his eyes.

He props himself against the wall and gropes for the container of T-Butoxilina. He tries to retrieve it from an inner pocket, only to find the syringe needle bent in half.

As he lies there, exhausted and in pain, he surveys the room. He sees Blass and his ruined hands, Flexibee unconscious, his welfare hands, and the black boxes.

After a while, he rises and swings the damaged door shut.

INT. POOL HALL

SOME TIME LATER

Maltex is in a pool hall playing against some man.

Maltex stands beside the pool table, while his opponent breaks. People are watching, Cabbie is among them.

No balls sink. The opponent cringes.

A smile creeps across Maltex's face. He circles the table, surveying each possible shot carefully.

He chooses one vantage point and aims.

TIGHT ON...

Maltex's hands as he holds his cue stick.

His hands are slim, delicate. A woman's. Flexibee's.

On the right one, there is a duplicate of the tattoo that was on his original hands. The tattoo that he refused to put on the old welfare hands.

TIGHT ON...

The cue ball as the cue stick hits it solidly.

                              FADE TO BLACK.
                    The End

www.ingramcontent.com/pod-product-compliance
Lightning Source LLC
Chambersburg PA
CBHW050455110726
47899CB00003B/951